WHEREVER THE ROAD TAKES US

K. MARTIN

www.TrueVinePublishing.org

Wherever the Road Takes Us
By: Kyjuan Martin

Published by True Vine Publishing Co.
P.O. Box 22448
Nashville, TN 37202
www.TrueVinePublishing.org

ISBN: 978-1-7366672-5-5
Copyright © 2021 by Kyjuan Martin

All rights reserved. No part of this book may be reproduced, scanned, or distributed in any printed or electronic form without permission. Please do not participate in or encourage piracy of copyrighted materials in violation of the author's rights.

Prologue:

The gentle wind breezed past my wrinkled skin and through the grass beneath me. I squinted to get a glimpse of the sun creeping below the grey sky and above the horizon. The setting did the courtesy of reminding me of a time when life was different. Long ago when the grass wasn't green, the wind was cold, and the sun never showed itself. It's become a bit of a struggle to stand and make my way to my front door, due to my declining years of course, but I managed. Making my way through our living room, a flicker of light from my peripheral caught my attention. My hands grabbed the picture frame and I analyzed it sentimentally. It was the four of us sitting down in that old diner, laughing until we couldn't breathe anymore. It was a million years ago, yet my feelings indicated that these events were yesterday. And of all the things going on in this picture, she stood above them all. The tenderness of her smile and the life in her eyes. The ones which changed my life.

To everyone who never had a chance.

Wherever The Road Takes Us

Part 1

Chapter 1

Sunlight crept through the window blinds as my eyes opened. I rose out of bed slowly, pushing the dark grey sheets away and mentally preparing myself for another day of "Jaxson's Fantastic Life." Loaded to the top with a hypocritical and alcoholic dad, who has a hard time keeping his hands to himself. And a narcissistic, gullible, and pitiful mother. She may be a college graduate but don't let that fool you; she's as simple as simpletons get. These two magnificent people are my foster parents. Ladies and gentlemen, meet Foster Care's best stab at,

"Doing their job."

Looking in the mirror, I spread the light blue toothpaste across my toothbrush and scrubbed it along my teeth, making sure to move up and down, as well as side to side. When done, I spat out the paste, washed my curly hair, moisturized my caramel skin, and then proceeded to get dressed for school. I hoped one day I'd be met with the smell of breakfast as I stepped down the rosewood staircase. And every day I met nothing except the same damn creaks in every step. They were consistently loud, irritating, and made me consider trying out the window for a change.

Entering the kitchen, I immediately noticed a collection of empty beer bottles spread across the marble counter. "Mondays," I mumbled, picking them up and disposing of them in the dark grey trash can nearby. That explained why Mark was nowhere to be found. However, the question still lingered, 'Where's Julia?' Then a thought came across my mind, "Do I care?" The black, round bowl scraped against the wooden cabinet's interior as I pulled it out in preparation for a bowl of cereal. Savoring the crunch of Honey Nut Cheerios, I stared at my dark blue Under Armour backpack.

Time for another day of Sycamore High School, which wasn't that bad. Unlike the other kids, I rushed to get ready for school and dreaded going home. The oven clock read 8:43. I prayed it was wrong, because school started at 9:00 and I wasn't even done with breakfast. Flipping out my phone, it read 8:44. I gobbled down a few more spoonsful of cereal before draining the milk in the sink, and pushing what was left of the soggy cereal into the garbage can.

After promptly exiting through the back door, I realized the chance of me being late to class was becoming more and more of a reality while I was walking down the broad sidewalk. That wouldn't be the case if I had a car. I had the license, but when you don't have parents who care, that doesn't matter. The autumn breeze made me lose my train of thought as it slowly seeped its way through the leaves. There was something different about today; I just couldn't put my finger on it. It was as if no one in the world existed on this short walk to school, and the sun seemed to only care about me. There was something freeing about these kinds of moments to me, and instead of questioning it, I began to simply enjoy it. This was short-lived when a ring, followed by an annoying vibration, came from my right pocket.

Before I even reached into my pocket, I knew who it was. "Jimmy Delgado," I thought to myself with a smirk. See, some people like to call us "Partners in Crime," and we wish just about everyone else in the world would. I've been running with Jimmy since 7th grade. We've gone as far from terrorizing our next-door neighbors to trying the people down the block for once, which wasn't as satisfying as we thought it would be. Jimmy has always been a constant in my life. He was a redhead, with freckles covering both of his cheeks. From what I knew, Jimmy was a mix of European and Mexican; his mom being Mexican and his dad being European.

He came from a single-parent household with his mother, who probably has the biggest heart I've ever seen. She's even let me spend the night at Jimmy's house, possibly more times than she should've, when I got kicked out by my "parents." And as far as his father, Jimmy avoids that topic. I've tried to bring it up a couple of times in the past, and whenever I did, he just changed the subject. The only thing I knew was that his father was a big boxer at one point. Which, I can infer, is why Jimmy literally eats, sleep, and breathes boxing. I guess he's to thank for my physique, because I wouldn't have exercised if he hadn't made me join the school's boxing team: Sycamore's Shockers. Escaping my thoughts, I retrieved my phone from my pocket and finally answered.

"Hello."

"Yo Jax, you heading to school?"

"Where else would I be heading on a Monday morning?"

"I don't know, maybe the tracks perhaps?"

The tracks - somewhat of a safe zone for the teenagers of Sycamore, Illinois. Last year the graduating class of seniors decorated and cleaned out two abandoned freight trains. They were abandoned by a rail service that had been shut down years ago. It's mainly used as a safe space for teens to do frankly whatever they want, and it's crazy to think that not that many people know about it.

"Are you just trying to get out of first-period or are you taking a day off?" I questioned.

"The four of us will be taking a day off."

"Four?" Jimmy and I alone made two, and I'm pretty sure his girlfriend Angela was going to be tagging along.

"Who's the fourth?

"One Victoria Summers."

Knowing Jimmy, I was 95% sure he said this with a smile on his face. Victoria, who Jimmy thinks I've had a crush on since freshman year, is a girl who I've always wanted to talk to more. And just so coincidentally she's best friends with Angela, who is Jimmy's current girlfriend. Being around Victoria wasn't the reason I decided to take Jimmy up on this offer; at least for the most part it wasn't. What persuaded me the most was that the days of Jimmy and I painting the town red were coming to an end, and he had no idea. Even as close as we were, he was unaware of my intentions.

The intention to attempt to take control of my life. Which was a nice way of saying simply running away. "Yo Jaxson, you there?" His voice snapped me out of my thoughts instantly. I took a deep breath and asked, "Where are you now?"

The clock now read 9:13, exactly thirteen minutes after the time Jimmy swore he'd be here. Jimmy Delgado is the only person I know who consistently picks a time to match his convenience, and still manages to be late. This gave me more time to admire the inside of Joe's Diner. Its walls were covered with chipped light blue paint. I was considering ordering breakfast, and probably would have done if I hadn't recognized the horrible screech of Jimmy's front tires pull up in the driveway. He seriously needed to get those checked out. I studied the rusted teal walls and the marble tables before I rose from my leather seat and headed towards the door. "Now hold up; don't be in such a rush to leave just yet."

I recognized the voice immediately. Old man Joe. Joe's around his early fifties but I like to make him feel like he's a hundred. Joe's always been good to me, and I'm pretty sure it's because he's one of the few people who knows how life is for me at home. He learned about it when the Palmer family had the infamous trip to his diner one night, years ago. It's undoubtedly still the worst night Mark has ruined. I grinned before turning around.

"Old man Joe!" I shouted, hoping he wouldn't wonder why I wasn't in school.

"Shouldn't you be in school by now?"

"Shouldn't you be retired by now?" I remarked.

"Nice one," he smirked. He stepped a bit closer.

"But seriously, how are you doing nowadays?" he said.

"I'm alright," I replied.

He moved in a bit closer and lowered his voice, in order to prevent anyone from hearing the words he would say next. "Well, if you ever need anything-"

"You're always here, I know I know," I cut him off. He repeated the statement every time we crossed paths. That didn't mean I was unappreciative of it. I walked towards the door and grabbed its steel handle.

"Thanks Joe, it means a lot. And tell Katherine I said Hi."

"Will do; be safe out there Jaxson." I nodded my head, exiting the diner. The redness of Jimmy's GMC truck stuck out like a sore thumb in the driveway. Jimmy's face lit up the moment he spotted me. Angela was too busy with what seemed to be finding a radio station to notice my approach. I couldn't help my eyes as they wandered right past the two and on to the hazel-eyed, lightly brown-haired, freckled face in the backseat, gazing out of the back window.

Every step I took was accompanied by a bit of nervousness and somewhat excitement. Victoria Summers; I've always seen her as a "Wonder Girl." We've talked before, and we've always known of each other, we've just never really hung out. The last time I talked to her was sophomore year. The two of us were partnered for a presentation in English. From what I remember we bombed it badly.

It wasn't long before I made my way to the back door and opened it. There she was. Her caramel skin, covered by a bright yellow, long-sleeve hoodie and a pair of light ripped jeans. Her eyes the color of spring leaves, and a sweet perfume which floated across the black car seats and into my nostrils.

I tried my best not to look for too long as she looked over, back at me. "Hey," followed with a simple smile. However, for some reason it felt like much more. "Hi," I did my best not to stumble over my words. After sitting down, I immediately began to rethink a million different approaches I could've gone through with besides a simple "Hey." First impressions are everything, after all. After I greeted Jimmy and Angela, the car ride fell silent, and the only noises being made were from the dangling of Jimmy's boxing necklace hanging from his interior window and the occasional bump in the road.

Throughout the duration of the ten-minute ride, I found myself gazing out of my passenger window. Artless scenery passed me by and now, instead of stopping in the old desolate junkyard, I was hoping we ended up somewhere thousands of miles from here. It didn't matter where or how far, as long as it wasn't this one-star town. "Oh, babe look!" Angela propped herself up in her seat, releasing some of her blond hair from being squished in between her back and the seat. "There was another robbery last night." She'd held up her phone to show him, but Jimmy hadn't seemed the least bit interested.

The car came to a halt without me noticing it. When we exited the car, Jimmy and Angela wasted no time bundling up, and they began to walk around the junkyard. His arm wrapped around her shoulder and over her light purple tank top. He pulled her closer and whispered something in her ear that broke her out into laughter. The two weren't like most teenage couples. They didn't date for a couple of months and break up once every two-three weeks. No, those two were consistent, which is pretty rare nowadays.

We followed them around the abandoned junkyard and into the forest behind. The crunching of the leaves underneath us seemed to be amplified by the silence. Halfway through the walk Angela slipped, possibly because of the uneven ground, and almost fell on a log. Lucky for her, Jimmy caught her. She then proceeded to make a big deal about it, as if she actually did slip and fall onto the log. As Jimmy and Angela got caught up in their ramblings I heard a voice to my left that snapped me out of my amusement. "Isn't it beautiful?" My attention shifted over to Victoria, taking notice of her tanned skin as she gazed upwards.

Out of curiosity, I decided to join her and look up. The various colors of the autumn trees lit up the wooden area. The feel of the breeze and slight shine of the sun, covered by trees, complemented it all so well. If it wasn't for her, my view would've still been filled with nothing but rough tree bark. "Yeah, it is; wow, I never really noticed it before. Is it always like this?" I asked, taking a look at her. "Unfortunately, no. And when it is, most people don't even notice it," she answered with an elegant smile, never breaking her gaze from what was above her.

"I'll keep that in my mind." A few minutes later we reached a slight clearing in the woods, where the two deserted train cars were located.

The orange paint from years prior was beginning to fall off the old abandoned train cars, which were still sitting on tracks that were shut down years ago. "Ladies and gentlemen. Here we are!" Jimmy exclaimed as he threw his arms in the air as if he was presenting some sort of circus or carnival. Angela came up behind him and wrapped her arms around him, and silently whispered something in his ear. Her blonde hair was covering his left shoulder. He turned around and held her face as the couple began to peck each other's lips multiple times.

"Get a train," I spoke up as the giggling couple practically fell into one of the train cars. Now it was just me and Victoria. I'll admit, I was pretty nervous, yet at the same time I was kind of glad. "Is it just me or is this place overrated?" I questioned, attempting to spark a conversation. "Trust me, it's not just you," she admitted. "Although, the view is pretty good," she continued. Looking down the stone-covered tracks led me to a mediocre view of the horizon. "I guess it's alright."

"No," she countered. "The tracks are alright, but it's beyond the tracks that's worth the trip," she said, working her way past the tracks and into the woods beyond the clearing. She signaled for me to follow her. After listening to the muffled laughter of the couple to my right I decided there were better places to be, and I quickly made my way towards her to see what she was talking about. She made her way through the trees, bypassing the rough bark, and at a speed that caused her hair to fly in the wind.

"You know the way back, right?" I shouted out of genuine concern, pushing a low branch out of my way.

"I'm pretty sure I do," she answered, laughing. "Pretty sure?!"

"You're not going to want to go back anyway." The words escaped her mouth with humor.

Now, I was a bit intrigued to see where this was going. A faint noise began to come from in front of us. The closer we got, the more I recognized it as the sound of water rushing down a stream. She stopped her feet abruptly once she came across another clearing in front of her. I slowed my jog in anticipation of my stop.

"Now this is far more interesting than sitting around in some old freight trains."

This clearing wasn't long and narrow like the one with the tracks. It was circular, and it felt like somewhat of a safe secure location. It was medium-sized, with most of the room being taken up by the beautiful pond that was located dead in the center of it. The water was crystal clear, the stones were white, and the grass was littered with just a few beautiful, brightly colored flowers. It was done so well that, if I hadn't known any better, I would have believed she had organized it all by herself.

"I can't disagree with you there." She found herself a spot in the grass. Picking up a couple of stones, she dusted them off and began to gracefully toss them into the water body.

"So, do you come here often?" I asked, sitting down and picking up a few of my own.

"Only when I'm bored enough or if I need space to daydream."

"Daydream? You have a set place just for daydreaming?" I chuckled, slightly teasing her.

"What? You know, there are probably tons of other people who do it too," she insisted back.

"For your sake I hope there are." After I said this she leaned over a bit and nudged my shoulder with hers. We both took a second to laugh at this. Her laugh was light, yet oddly delightful to hear.

"So, what is it that you think about?"

"Umm...nothing important," she said.

"No. If you have an entirely safe space for these thoughts of yours, I'm pretty sure they're important." She looked at me and I could infer that she was nervous about opening up whatever was going on in that head of hers. "Well," she then retracted her legs and wrapped her arms around them, holding them tightly against her chest, "stories. I know how it sounds, but everyone has complex lives with their own problems, mistakes, and stories. And half of the time I think we're too caught up in our own to realize that."

I stayed there for a minute staring at her just in a state of astonishment, because I too was someone who had never thought of things that way. It was 10:00 am; I should've been on my way to my locker and getting ready for second-period U.S. History by now. Yet here I was, sitting in the middle of the woods, with a girl I'd barely ever talked to, and I had just learned something that school had never taught me.

"Yeah look. I know it's pretty stupi-" she started, beginning to get up.

I cut her off with a "No," before she could finish, and she returned to her position.

"I've never actually thought of it that way before."

I looked into her colored eyes as she nervously looked back. My guess was she hasn't told many people that. The next few words were selfish; only because of my intention of leaving town. Even so, I couldn't find the strength to stop my next few words. "Do you want to hang out sometime?"

Chapter 2

The thoughts of yesterday trapped me in a daydream, assisting me in passing time through another one of Ms. Marie's unbearable lectures. The seemingly mystical image of Victoria locked itself in my head. I tapped my pencil against the tabletop of my desk more as the clock came closer to hitting 3:45. Jimmy leaned and whispered, "Looks like someone's excited to get some alone time with V." I nudged him over a bit with my shoulder and he laughed in response. As much as I wanted to ignore his comment, it was true. Victoria and I planned on hanging out for a bit after school today. All I had to do now was meet her at her locker after school ended.

The bell satisfied my ears as I jerked out of my seat, gathering my belongings, and headed for the door. "Not so fast, you two." The words could've been meant for anyone, literally anyone, in the room. Nevertheless, it took no genius to know their targets. The spruce wood door in front of me made the idea of making a run for it very tempting. It most likely wasn't worse than dealing with her detention, which was equivalent to her normal class period. Turning around, I mentally prepared myself for whatever was to come.

Ms. Marie stared down Jimmy and I with her beady, wrinkled eyes through her cat's-eye glasses. She cleared her throat as we approached. "I found it very interesting how both of you were absent yesterday. Now, I would like to give you the benefit of the doubt and say that these two absences aren't connected. I guess a little reassurance would be nice." She folded her arms in a bundle and looked at us, awaiting our reasoning. Lying wasn't exactly my strong suit, but if it came down to getting out of detention, I would do my best.

"I came down with a cold yesterday. It wasn't that bad; I just didn't want to risk spreading it to anyone else," I pleaded. I was pretty sure she didn't believe my alibi. It didn't matter now. Her attention was now on Jimmy.

"I went over to check on Jaxson, and I ended up catching it as well," he responded, scratching his head with his signature grin. I took a deep breath, closed my eyes, and couldn't believe how horrible one could be at lying. "So you both were sick, is what I'm hearing?" The slight curve of her head and squinting of her eyes clarified that she didn't believe a word we uttered.

"Yes," shot out of our mouths identically.

"Hmm. Okay. You may leave." Her face displayed nothing besides skepticism as she fixed her glasses back on top of her nose and sat back down at her desk.

"Really? You caught a cold from me?" I said as soon as we closed the classroom door behind us.

"Hey, it was either that or my dog died bro."

"You don't even have a dog."

"Exactly, I was limited on options," he said, as if there were no better options. "Whatever man, I'll catch you later." I split off from him and made my way to my locker on the second floor near the bottom of the stairwell. My black G-Shock watch read 3:54. Once I was done packing my books, I made my way up another floor in search of locker number #6547. The hallway fluttered with people stepping across the white vinyl flooring. However, none stood out like her.

She needed a bit of support from her toes to retrieve whatever she needed from the back of her locker. Her golden-brown hair fell over her brown leather jacket. Her jeans were dark blue and today she had on a light green crew neck. My steps to her were filled with nervousness; luckily for me, she was facing the opposite direction. "Hey," her body instantly jolted forward in a frightened manner. She whirled around and the shock on her face wore off once she realized it was me. She palmed her face, which smushed the awkward smile hidden beneath. As much as I tried to refrain from doing so, I couldn't help but laugh at her reaction.

"Sorry, I didn't mean to startle you."

"No, you're fine. I've just been a little jumpy today," she said, relinquishing the rest of her embarrassment from her system.

"So, are you ready to head out?" I asked.

"I've been ready since homeroom."

"So where exactly are we heading Mr. Palmer?" I was assuming she said that with the intent of making fun of my last name, which she accomplished.

"Well, Victoria–"

"Just call me Vicky," she interrupted, "It feels weird when people call me by my full name."

"Well, Victoria Summers," I said, and she rolled her eyes with a cute smirk.

"Usually after school, I go down to Joe's and get a burger or two," I said, looking both ways up and down the road ahead.

"Wait, did you say a burger or two?"

"Yep."

"Ohh so you're one of *those* guys," she said, emphasizing the word those.

"And what exactly does that mean?"

"Oh, you know, the ones who have no limit when it comes down to food consumption."

"Very funny," I said sarcastically. "And what type of girl are you?"

"You'll find out eventually." Her statement left me in a bit of intriguing wonder.

***

The distance between us and the diner became smaller and smaller. I sped up just enough to reach the door before her. Opening it, I stepped back, giving her enough room to enter. Readjusting her book bag she said, "Thank you," and did so. She moved towards the booth in the back right-hand corner of the restaurant. The seat had a huge window to the right of it, giving us a clear view of the street. She took a seat, facing the door, and I sat across from her.

When we finished dropping our bags on the floor a familiar, middle-aged, black-haired waitress appeared at our table. She wore a white and light blue waitress outfit accompanied by a notepad and a welcoming smile.

"If it isn't my favorite customer," she greeted.

"And if it isn't the best waitress in Sycamore," I replied.

She looked at Victoria. "Victoria, meet Katherine," I said, motioning towards the waitress.

"She's been serving me for as long as I can remember."

Victoria extended her hand towards Katherine and said, "Well, it's nice to meet you."

Katherine extended hers and the two shook hands as she replied with, "Likewise."

"So what can I get for you two today?"

"The usual for me," I said

"Okay, so that'll be one double cheeseburger with a side of cheese fries and a vanilla milkshake," she reported from memory.

"And how about you, young lady?" she said to Victoria.

Victoria settled with an order of chicken nuggets, fries, and a strawberry lemonade. After that, Katherine made her way to the kitchen. Propping herself up in her seat, Victoria looked directly into my eyes. She squinted and searched my eyes as if they clue to some sort of mystery.

"So what's your story?" She sat up in her seat, folded her hands, and squinted her eyes as she began her interrogation.

I gave her a puzzled look, "What do you mean?"

"Your story," she said, relaxing in her seat and crossing her arms. "Everyone has one."

"I was born in Chicago, lived there until I was ten. The city got worse, so my parents decided to relocate." And there it was - my first lie. It was white and rehearsed, not that it made the process any easier.

"Why Sycamore? Why not a bit farther? If you don't mind me asking."

"I like to think it was more of a spontaneous decision, instead of a well thought out one."

"Do you have any siblings?" she questioned.

These words caught me off guard. The answer was yes, and the answer I wanted to tell her was yes.

"No, just me. I've always wanted one, if we're being honest."

"Trust me, you don't," she said.

"So. I'm guessing you're not the only child?"

"No, I'm not," she rolled her eyes, "unfortunately."

"How many do you have?"

"Two brothers, one sister."

"What ages?"

"My older brother is 19, my younger brother is 15, and my younger sister is 13." Jeez, four teenagers at once, I pitied the parents. "And we're the Summers!" she exclaimed, throwing her hands in the air pretending to be excited. Although this was corny and overused, seeing her do it was pretty cute and I found myself laughing.

"You know, I've never told you this, mainly because we've never talked that much. But I've always liked that last name," I said.

"What about it?"

"I honestly don't know, I've always found it…" I struggled to find the words, "satisfying."

She began to squint her eyes and stare at me as if she was in deep thought.

"So, Ms. Summers, how do you like to spend *your* time?" I asked her out of curiosity.

"Well," she paused to think, "I used to spend a lot of time writing. It's been awhile though."

"Were you any good?"

"I was ahead of my time," she claimed with confidence.

There was her confidence that enticed me so much. "And what about you? Any hidden talents I should know about?" she leaned forward a bit.

"I mean, I used to draw a bit," I said, scratching my head.

She began to sit back, "Aweee, a modern-day Picasso, huh?"

"Initially I would've compared my skills to a 1st grader but I like that title much better." The sounds of Katherine's heels clicking against the ground was equivalent to music to my ears. I knew exactly what that meant. The food was on its way.

"Why're you smiling so hard?" asked Victoria, snapping me out of my thoughts.

"You'll see."

"Here you!" Katherine laid two lovely plates of food down in front of us. One with my double cheeseburger with everything on it and an order of cheese fries in front of me. The other with Victoria's order of chicken nuggets and fries. After placing down my vanilla milkshake with extra whipped cream next to me, she gave Victoria her lemonade. "Enjoy your meal," she cheered before disappearing behind the counter and into the kitchen. There wasn't a day in history where Katherine forgot to bring her smile to work.

I looked across from me at Victoria, who was focused on her plate. But this time something was different - for the first time the sun was shining through the windows to my right, and I saw her. I saw her in the light. And for a second, I'll admit, I was caught in a daze. As she fixed her hair behind her left ear, I noticed how the sunlight shimmered down on her tanned skin and how brightly her hazel eyes reflected it. She truly was beautiful, and I planned on telling her that eventually.

"So I see you have a love for cheese," she said, picking up one of her nuggets.

"The cheese fries gave it away," she spoke up.

"Everything's better with cheese," I protested while pointing one at her.

"Well, I can't argue with that." We both took a break from talking to start our meals.

"So let me get this straight. You're okay with the food on your plate touching?"

"Look, if it were my choice, I would put every meal I ate in a blender and eat it like that," I replied, standing firmly behind my beliefs. She held her hands over her mouth as if she were about to throw up. "I'll be the one to tell you. That is not, and I repeat, IS NOT okay," she argued. "But don't worry - there are many other people like me who're here to get you the help you deserve." She placed a hand on my shoulder to amplify her role-playing even more.

    I told her I'd drop her off, mainly just to spend some more time with her. As we walked down the cracked sidewalk, I learned a lot about her. Contrary to most people my age, Vicky was interesting.

    She loved spring and hated winter, her favorite color was baby blue, and she loved it even more if it was in glitter. Alice, which was her mother's name, was her middle name. Her birthday was in May, she hated the scent of bubblegum, and couldn't live without a bag of peanut M&M's. It wasn't long before we arrived at her doorstep. Surprisingly, her house was only about a mile or so from mine. In between our laughter we both began to hear a concerning sound come from the inside of her house. I examined the two-floor house with its stucco exterior. The sound of an argument coming from inside could be heard the closer we got to it. For the first time, her eyes were staring at the ground instead of whatever was in front of or above her. We stopped in front of her house. "Hey, I never actually got your number," I said, attempting to take her mind off it.

    "Oh, I'm sorry. Give me your phone, I'll put it in for you." I reached in my pocket and pulled out my smartphone for her. After a few seconds of typing she held it up and took a selfie of her holding up the peace sign. She held it out for me to retrieve and said, "You better use it."

    "Oh trust me. I will," I responded, in my best attempt of a flirty tone. She waved at me one last time with a smile as she dug into her pockets for what I presumed to be her house keys. I began to walk home, eventually putting my headphones in to make the walk more enjoyable. Approaching the house I noticed the old blue SUV parked outside. This signified that Mark and Julia were back home. Through the windows I could make out the kitchen light that was on.

Mark, who was usually sitting in the chair blasting his football game and drinking a beer, was nowhere to be found. That was out of routine. "Your dinner's in the fridge," was the first thing I'd heard Julia say all day. This time she didn't do her occasional muttering of words and then walking off. She stood by the kitchen entrance, staring at me as if something was wrong. Julia's black hair fell behind the velvet shirt she was wearing. Her eyes were still dark brown, but her face had received a few more wrinkles since I'd first met her. "I'm fine," I said. The words "Are you sure?" rung from the kitchen. "Yes, I'm sure." I could still feel her glare on me as I walked up the stairs.

After dropping my book bag by the door and flopping down on my bed, I gazed at the ceiling above me. Today wasn't that bad, I thought to myself. It was the first time I'd said that in a while and genuinely meant it. My phone buzzed. I reached over to see what it was. A total of $500 had been deposited into my bank account. The one which no one else knew about. I got a text afterward.

Sorry I can't be with you tomorrow, but here's an early birthday present.

The message came from Benjamin. Which was a horrible fake name, though I never put much effort into it anyway.

Chapter 3

September 25th. This was a normal day to most, but it only came around once a year for me. Today was my eighteenth birthday. Not many people know that, because I'd never exactly made it public information after all. Although it's hard to admit, if there was one day where Mark and Julia attempted to play their part, it was today. Every year in the Palmer house for my birthday there was a tradition: Julia would bake a cake and Mark would give me a pat on the back - that is, if he wasn't wasted of course. I expected this when I arrived home from school. So, when I woke up and realized that neither of them was home, I knew my anticipation would lead to disappointment.

One other thing about the Palmers was that sometimes they would just disappear randomly for a day or two and wouldn't say anything. This happened seldomly, but never had it aligned with my birthday. This did impact my emotions a bit, yet after living with these people for so many years, it was nothing that couldn't be brushed off. I decided to take the day to do separate things anyway. Since it was a Friday, I figured that there was a good chance I'd have an entire weekend to myself. After finalizing this decision, I texted both Jimmy and Victoria to inform them I wouldn't be attending school today.

Jimmy, who knew it was my birthday, replied saying he'd pick me up after school to celebrate. And as for

Vicky, she never responded, which was weird because she was always on her phone in the morning. The constant realization that I was now eighteen replayed in my head over and over in my mind as I tried not to step on the cracks embedded into the cement. No matter how old I get I'll never stop playing this; what some would call a "childish" game.

I scanned the book bag aisle of Walmart, searching for a duffel bag or even a suitcase of some sort hoping it would be there. It took a small amount of looking before I stumbled upon an all-black one. Its price tag read $17:00. I tossed it in the cart and went off to see if there were any jackets or jeans on sale. I made sure to grab everything in shades of black or dark gray, as I just preferred them over brighter colors. It wasn't always this way. In my pre-adolescent years I did nothing but draw on paper, books, and even the walls at times. Walking by a section filled with packs of crayons and colored pencils reminded me of this. But just like damn near everything else, Mark had ruined that as well.

A group complete with a mother, father, teenage girl, and a preschool boy stood in front of me in line. The boy played with a plastic yellow toy plane. I watched as he swung around wildly, replicating the buzz of a plane engine through his lips. His mother declared that he should stop, but she was too occupied to do it herself and make sure of it. Eventually he knocked a couple of candy bars off the counter during one of his spins.

"MICHAEL!" shouted his mother, quickly grabbing him out of embarrassment.

Kneeling down I began to help her stack the bars back on the shelf properly.

"Sorry," she apologized, trying to make light of the situation.

"He gets a little clumsy sometimes."

"No, it's fine. Kids will be kids after all."

I liked this woman. Mainly because she reminded me of my mom, and no, not Julia. My actual mother, the one I'll sadly never see again. After placing the items back on their shelves, I wished her farewell and returned to my spot in line. The total came out to $45.78, which was $5 above what I'd expected. Exiting the store I pulled out my phone. The usual news and Snapchat notifications met me; however, there was still no response from Vicky. The time now read 1:27. I was pretty sure she, along with everyone else, was in class. Arriving home, I moved towards the kitchen and started shuffling through wooden drawers, moving miscellaneous objects out of the way until my eyes found the grey and yellow striped slotted screwdriver. I grabbed it, went upstairs to my room, and opened my closet.

I reached in, turned on the light, and shuffled all of my clothes lying around or hanging up inside to the right. The spot on the floor stood out compared to every other floor tile. It was dented, which was done purposefully. Kneeling, I wedged the screwdriver in between the tiles and pried it open. It's been over six months and I've just recently been able to find the compartment consistently. A fake ID that put me as 21-year-old Jesse Plummer (courtesy of Riley Henkins), around $750 in cash, a small box of non-perishable food items, and now a duffel bag. Digging further into the pile, I found an old family photo. It's one of the few things I kept that reminded me of my life. My former one, at least. I missed those times more than anything. Back when my mom would tuck me into bed at night and tell me how much she loved me. Back when everything was simple and sweet. I brushed my thumb across their smiling faces as if I could actually touch their faces. It's no secret how pointless the act was, but nonetheless it still comforted me.

After putting the wooden plank back in place I stood to my feet, shut the closet door, and took a nice long stare at my room. What was irritating about it was how empty it felt. I had no posters or fun pictures of me and my friends laying around. Hell, I didn't even have paint on the walls, they were still white after all this time. Surprisingly, this was one of the things that bothered me the most. I feel like I've wasted a lot of time that I can't get back. Oh well, no point in sulking now. Turning on the stovetop I initiated my cabinet search for whatever canned food I'd be diving into today, I didn't even bother with the refrigerator, because I was quite sure it was empty. After shuffling around the dust with my fingertips I felt a can in the back.

Pulling it out, I found an old can of ravioli. "Looks like we've got a winner." That should hold me over till everyone got out of school. After I finished heating my meal, I took it to the couch, flipped through the channels, and settled on an episode of Full House. I had about an hour and a half to kill before school ended for my peers.

"She didn't come to school today and Angela hasn't heard from her either." With the sound of traffic in the background I struggled to hear him through my phone. I stopped my walk.

"What do you mean?"

"She didn't attend school today."

"Are you sure?"

"If Angela says she wasn't there, then she wasn't. Trust me. If anyone knew anything about Vicky's whereabouts, it would be her."

If my memory served me correctly, I wasn't far from where she lived.

"Maybe I should drop by her house and check on her."

"Bold move."

"We'll be waiting for you two at Joe's," yelled Angela, who I guess was trying to make sure I could hear her. "I'll be there as soon as I can." After ending the phone call I took a left and started making my way towards her house. My hand paused right as I was about to knock my fist upon the light brown door. I couldn't help the feeling of anxiety as it spread around my stomach.

Not long after banging upon the door, a tall, blonde-haired white man answered the door shortly afterward. He was wearing a blue button-after all with dress pants and a slick black belt that failed at restraining his belly.

"Hello, how may I help you this evening?" He possessed a professional tone.

"Good evening, Sir, I'm a friend of Victoria's. Is she home?" I asked.

When I asked this his eyebrows furrowed, "I'm sorry, I think you've got the wrong house." I took a step back and looked at the house, replaying the scene of me dropping her off in my head.

"I'm sure this is it," I reassured him.

"We don't know anyone named Victoria, son."

"But-"

"Have a nice day," he said, closing the door in my face abruptly.

None of the other houses on the block looked like the one I'd walked her home to; this had it be it. Either I didn't pay close enough attention that day or she lied to me. No. I was sure this was it. So why did she lie? I flipped out my phone and sent Jimmy a text letting him know that I was on my way.

He replied a few moments later.

Good because guess who just got here......VICKAYYYYYY

A shock of nervousness rushed down my spine, increasing the pace of my heartbeat. Reaching for the handle of the diner's door I didn't know what to say or how to feel. I wanted to know why she'd felt the need to lie. Confronting her about it was something that had to be done; just not now. This wasn't the place nor was it the time. When opening the door, it was pretty noticeable how big the crowd was compared to most nights. And then, in an instant, everyone stopped talking when I entered and turned their attention towards me. All types of people in different shapes and sizes; some were noticeable from school and others I knew from around. It was a small town after all. "SURPRISE!" cheered every person in the room, some holding up drinks to me and others slapping me on the back. This had old man Joe and Jimmy Delgado's name all over it.

Even with what I'd just discovered I couldn't help but smile at this. Nothing like this had happened to me in years. Not since Mom and Dad took me to that amusement park. They let me eat cotton candy all day long and even allowed me to go on my first rollercoaster. Mom was skeptical of it the entire time, but Dad didn't seem to mind. Noah even told me that it was my first step towards being a man. And when I finally got off, they were all standing up with their hands cupped over their mouths screaming and waving at me, sort of like how Jim, Vicky, and Angela were. I received a lot of pats on the back and happy birthdays while making my way to their seat.

The process of thanking as many people as I could was slightly tedious but heartwarming nonetheless. Jimmy extended his hand and when I made it to their table. He pulled me in close and wrapped an arm around me, "Happy Birthday Brother." Hearing him say this meant more than everyone else before me. I remembered when it was my first birthday after I was adopted. He was one of the only people I knew and yet he treated it as if it meant the world. That's a memory I'd always cherish. When he released me, Victoria stepped up and hugged me. I embraced all of her softness and warmth in my arms. She let go of me while leaving her hands to rest on my shoulders.

"Happy Birthday Jaxson," she said, with the prettiest smile I'd ever seen, and as much as I wanted to know why she lied, those eyes of hers caught me in a daze yet again. Before I could respond to her, Angela's voice rang from across the table saying, "And if someone didn't want to keep their birthday a secret so much, we could've planned something special. But Happy Birthday J." Jimmy flopped down on his seat next to Angela. "Damn, you're a man now." They might not have known this, nor would they believe it but this moment, before our "celebration" had even begun, had already made this my best birthday yet. And just when I thought it couldn't be any better, Katherine and Joe appeared from the kitchen with a large confetti cake - my favorite.

Her walk was slow and steady, being sure to balance the cake to the best of her ability. She set it down between the four of us and wished me a happy birthday while folding her hands and putting them under her chin. Shortly after, Joe ruffled my hair and teased me about how I would be getting my birthday licks the next time he saw me. A lot of great things were happening around me all at once, and I loved each of them. There was one in particular that stood out from the rest; the most memorable one. It wasn't when Joe pulled out an instant camera and snapped an unexpected photo of each of us. And it wasn't when we cut cake and it wasn't when

Jimmy slipped and fell while going to the washroom, although that was a close runner-up. It was simply mid-conversation between the four of us when Victoria moved a bit closer and inched her hand closer to mine.

I moved mine closer to hers and they met. Our fingers intertwined and we began holding hands. I looked up at her and watched her cheeks begin to burn. And I couldn't help but do the same. It wasn't that big of a deal, yet it felt like that. I felt extremely lucky. Not because I was finally sharing a connection with someone, but because it was with her. More people disappeared from the bar as the night grew closer to an end. Some granted me one last "Happy Birthday," while others just left. Around 7:00, Vicky said that she should start heading home. Hearing her say the word "home" made me wonder what she really meant by it.

At this point it was tempting to confront her about it. But, afraid that it would ruin the time we were having, I omitted the lingering question. She accepted my offer to walk her out and we both left the restaurant. Chill air grazed against my face when we opened the door. It was nothing a jacket couldn't handle. The sun had set, but thankfully the streetlights allowed us to survey our surroundings.

"Thank you; I had a really good time today," I said.

"Why're you thanking me?"

"I talked to Katherine, and she told me who the real mastermind behind this party was," I nudged her shoulder.

"It's your birthday, everyone deserves to feel special on their birthday."

"Well, usually that doesn't end up happening."

Nearing the edge of the sidewalk, our steps slowed before they came to a complete halt. Our bodies spiraled toward each other until our eyes met. I gazed into her colorful eyes. If it weren't creepy to do so I would never look away. Suddenly, some type of magnetic pull took over my legs and pulled me closer, and closer, towards her. Never breaking from her eyes, unless I peeked at her seductive lips. My palm found its way to her cheek while my fingers eased into her hair. I closed my eyes as the gap between our faces was almost nonexistent. When our lips finally met, it was as if she took away each of my senses. I couldn't hear, smell, see, or even think about anything else besides us in this wonderful, wonderful moment.

"Text me when you're home," I said. "I will." She then turned around, looked both ways, and crossed the street. I, on the other hand, didn't possess the strength to look at anything that wasn't her. Victoria Summers. There was just something about her. Maybe it was her sense of humor, or just merely the sound of her voice. I pondered it as I watched her become smaller and smaller in the distance. Whatever it was it was the cause of this sensation inside of me. One that I wanted to feel more and more of. Even though she was possibly hiding something from me, it would be hypocritical of me to bash her for it. Especially when I had some big secrets of my own. Heading back inside, I awaited the ride Jimmy promised before he dropped Angela off, which he delivered on after he grabbed one more slice of the cake. I swear he had more than anyone else.

On my way home, the memory of the family from the supermarket earlier crossed my mind again. I remembered a time, years ago, when I was a part of something like that. My brother and I would practically run wild in every supermarket we went in while my mother would be embarrassed, and my dad would be too busy hunting down sales to notice. My brother was only a few years older, and even though he was supposed to babysit me, half the time he ended up in more trouble than I did. It brought a smile to my face, accompanied by a tear to my eyes, to remember what it was like to be in an actual family again. One which lifts you and is always the first to be there during every softball game.

There's no such thing as a perfect pair of parents, but if that did exist, I feel like mine were the closest thing to it. It's funny how time changes everything. Here I am. Eighteen years-old with no idea what to do next. This void of simply not having a purpose. It was unbearable.

Chapter 4

The scent of her hair refused the idea of me moving from this couch. It was a week later, and Vicky was over. We'd been getting a lot closer lately, and I'd been enjoying it, a lot. We were halfway through some old cheesy 2000s rom-com when I looked over at her and asked if we could talk about something. "The other day, when I didn't hear from you, I decided to go to your house just before I made my way to Joe's." When I said this, her face dropped. Her smile faded away and she went from looking at me to studying the cheap couch we laid on top of.

"At first I was upset but–"

"I'm sorry," she interrupted me.

"I'm ashamed of where I live," she said.

She was always the straightforward type. Hearing her say this explained why she didn't seem to mind my house at all. Her tone became rather low, and I didn't like this change. Judging her for lying would be hypocritical, especially since I'd done a fair amount of that. I put one hand on her shoulder and lifted her cheek with the other.

"You don't have to feel embarrassed around me. Those kinds of things don't matter, and we have no control over it."

She looked at me. "I'm sorry. I don't have the most stable family and I didn't want you to know it."

"Trust me. I know what it's like."

"What does that mean?" she questioned.

"I'm. Well-" I considered telling her the truth. "I don't exactly have an exemplary relationship with my parents," I responded. For a moment we just lay there. It was nice to know there was someone else out there with similar problems.

"We've got each other," I said. The comment didn't come out as confidently as it should've. Even so, it was still genuine. That smile that I admired so much began to creep across her face.

"Is that a pinky promise?" she asked, displaying a huge smile. I palmed my face, unable to contain my laughter. "What?" she asked.

"I just wasn't aware that we were still in kindergarten," I replied.

"Hahahaha," she fake-laughed, implying that my joke wasn't funny.

She then held up a pinky and raised her eyebrow.

"Oh, you were serious."

I wrapped my pinky around hers, rolled my eyes, and said, "Promise." She leaned onto me and rested her head on my chest. And here it was, an actual good thing in my life. Someone funny, interesting, and possibly as troubled as I was when it came to the home situation. And yet here she was. Beautiful and at peace right here. She was wearing yet another sweater, as usual. This time it was light pink. She did have nice sweaters; it surprised me that she wore so many. And then I heard the worst noise known to mankind. The sharp, ear-piercing squeal of my Mark's tires pulling into the driveway. I jumped up a bit and she looked at me with fear.

"Is that-"

"Yes."

In an instant, I jolted up from the couch, grabbed her hand, and whispered, "Follow me." We didn't do much besides lay around, so the most I had to do was turn off the TV. I took her to the bathroom near the back of the house. There was a window we could sneak out through. I lifted the window and held her hand as she climbed through. That was around the time I heard the knob of the front door twist and it began to open. I began to make my way out through the window, starting with my right leg.

"Wait, you're not going to stay?" she asked.

"Hell No!" I whispered, as loudly as possible.

I was almost through when my foot slipped on the stool and I fell through the window onto the rough dirt. She stood over me, her hair falling under her face and the sun glistening off of her skin.

A smile curved on my mouth.

"I've got to admit, I'm enjoying the view."

"Shut up," she replied with a laugh, as she grabbed my arm and pulled me to my feet.

When I got up, I led her through the backyard, opened the back gate, and we ran to the end of the alley. When we were clear, we couldn't help but burst into laughter. In the moment it had been frightening. The aftermath, on the other hand, was pretty hilarious.

"So what's the plan now?" she asked me.

"It doesn't matter to me. As long as you're here." I reached for her hand.

She had both her hands wrapped around my left arm and then she rested her head on my shoulder. After that, we began to walk. We had no place in mind, we just followed the sidewalks. Shabbona Lake was a lake that Julia would take me to when I was a bit younger. Years ago when we had shared some sort of bond. It was somewhat of a long walk, but it was only noon and we had time.

The more I took in every detail around me, the more I realized how astonishing this scenery was. It looked way better than it did when I was younger, probably because my adolescent eyes weren't as keen as my current ones. Oddly enough, no matter what I saw, whether it was how the sun reflected off the water or the plethora of brightly colored flowers to my left, none of it shone as brightly as the girl to my right. I looked over and watched how she took pleasure in her surroundings. How her hand threaded softly through the shrub bushes and how the wind pushed her cotton candy scent back to me. The smell now only brought the image of her into my mind. I hadn't even seen her take a glance at her phone; I guess that was just the type of person she was.

She glanced over at me, and her smile ignited mine. We both looked back at the view in front of us and I pulled her a bit closer to me, and wrapped my hand around her shoulder. However, when I did this, I noticed she slightly jolted forward. That was weird, considering I'd barely touched her. I pushed my arm into the top of her back a tiny bit, as an experiment, and she did it again. Only this time it was a bit of a smaller movement. As if she was trying to pretend it didn't affect her. She wasn't saying anything at all. I moved back a bit to take a peek at her back through the collar of her sweater. The top of her back didn't match the rest of her skin tone.

Dark purple bruises littered the top of her back. Based on my experiences with Mark, I could infer that those had been there for a day or two. My heart dropped. I didn't know what to say, but above all, I was deeply concerned. I saw her head jerk to the right towards me. She opened her mouth and her eyes were red, as if she was about to burst into tears. "I'm so sorry. I'm so sorry. I'm sorry," she kept repeating as she began to cry. I didn't know what to say. Like an idiot, I watched her rise up and back away. My head began to fill with questions and concerns. "I have to go." She got up and walked away fiercely. "Victoria... wait!" The words finally made their way to my mouth, but it was beyond too late.

Cold and confusing were the only two words I could use to describe the walk home. She wasn't responding to any of my texts or calls. I couldn't shake the feeling that it was my fault. That if I had stopped prying, we'd still be sitting in the grass. Her mortified face. The look of sadness in her eyes. I closed my eyes and took a deep breath. The white door stood tall in front of me. Some type of reasoning would be needed for my arrival. Too focused on Victoria, I hadn't thought to make one before unlocking the door.

Mark sat on the couch. He was in the middle of rising from his seat, almost as if he'd been in anticipation of my arrival. A singular beer bottle sat on his table. This was a bit weird, because usually at this time he would be on his 3rd or 4th. He stood up and walked towards me slowly. "Jaxson," he said, and hearing him say that pissed me off a tad. I hated it when he said that. "Do you remember Paul?" he asked, edging closer. Paul is our next-door neighbor; he used to come over a lot and he seemed to be the only thing that kept Mark's attention off of me. Too bad I never saw him anymore. "Yeah, what about him?" I replied. He stopped in front of me. Julia stopped what she was doing, letting the dishes she held fall against the sink bottom. She held onto the countertop tightly. I knew what that meant.

Mark let off a sly smile and his mouth opened.

"You wouldn't believe what he saw today."

He placed a hand on my shoulder. I closed my eyes to brace myself for the right hook. There was no doubt it was coming. I just hoped he aimed for my stomach instead of my face. Seconds later and there was still nothing. Maybe he was just waiting for me to open my eyes.

He said, "Next time if you're going to have a girl over, just ask."

"What?" My eyes opened and stayed on him. Had I pricked my finger upon some poisonous plant back at the lake? Was I hallucinating? I mean I was pretty bummed out about what happened, but I didn't think my body's response would be this intense. "You heard me; now get ready for dinner." He backed up and went towards the hallway. Nope, I was perfectly normal. And that really did just happen. Julia kept on with cooking afterward. Meanwhile, I struggled to believe that that was all he'd said. In the past, he would beat me until I couldn't feel it anymore just because he simply felt like it. It confused me as to why he'd simply asked me not to do something again. This was something he'd never done before. Maybe he was on drugs.

Dinner was filled with a heavy, awkward silence, which was broken by Julia who asked, "So, who was she?" I looked over at her, thinking that there was no way she was asking about Victoria. Was she on drugs too?

"Yes you," she reassured me.

"Um…her name's Victoria."

"Oh. I used to know a Victoria in high school."

She told me this as if I was supposed to care.

"Do you remember her, Mark?"

He dropped his fork for a second and looked up in deep thought.

"Victoriaaaa…Conway. Victoria Conway, yea, she was my least favorite friend of yours."

"Oh wow, I always thought that would be Janet," Julia chuckled in response.

Why were they acting as if everything was okay?

"I have work to do," I interrupted their conversation, stood up, and made my way to my room, leaving my plate at the table.

The sound of a phone call broke the silence of my room as soon as my door closed behind me, leaving me no time to take in what had just happened. In hopes that it was Victoria, I flipped the phone out of my pocket. The caller ID displayed the word "Benjamin." The feeling of disappointment overcame me a bit; nevertheless, I was happy to hear from him.

A, "Yo J, you there?" came through the phone. Although a lot of inconveniences had been occurring lately, this brought a smile to my face. Hearing his voice reminded me of a better time.

"I haven't heard anyone call me that in a long time," I replied.

"That's because we haven't seen each other in forever."

"Yeah well, it feels that way," I said. I placed my back against the wall and slid down. Darkness congested the room. I wanted to ask him some kind of normal question about how he'd been or if he was dating anyone. Anything besides the tragedy that had struck us years ago. Sadly, I couldn't. I had to talk to someone who missed them as much as I did. Someone who knew that they existed. And how wonderful they were.

"So how's school? Have you met any girls yet?" he asked.

I rolled my eyes. He asked me this question every time we got on the phone.

"Actually, yes," I responded, knowing this answer would surprise him.

"Her name's Victoria. And she's.." I struggled to find a word that would give her justice, "unique," I finished.

"It's about time," he laughed.

A silence rang through the phone as he waited for me to respond. I didn't want to bring it up, but I just couldn't help myself.

"Do you think about them?" I asked, clenching my eyes closed.

"Every day," he replied.

Chapter 5

Fresh out of 3rd period Honors English, I was in the midst of retrieving my books for my next class when I spotted her. Even before Vicky and I began to spend time together more she always had a smile on her face. Rarely ever would she show up without her shine. And when she did, it was like someone had snatched the soul right out of her. And today was one of those days. This was my fault. Maybe I could've handled it differently. I stared for a couple of seconds, deciding how to approach the situation. She was nearing the end of the hallway. I reached for her, but a load of nervousness dragged down my shoulders. "Jaxson." A sweet voice froze my feet in place.

Mrs. Ryan was the school guidance counselor and for some reason she'd taken an interest in me since mid-freshman year. Truthfully, she had great reasons to worry. I turned around slowly, buying a little time before having to deal with whatever reason she had for stopping me. Her face lit up as always. I wasn't in the mood for her this time. The sweet sound of the bell rang through the halls. Saved by the bell indeed. "Looks like that's my cue," I smiled, turning around and scurrying away. My view of Victoria was officially ruined due to the crowded hall. This was probably for the best, considering I had no clue how to start my apology. Maybe a letter would suffice.

A tall man with a chocolate brown skin tone stood outside the door to my next class. He was around my height, with a buzz cut.

When I neared him, he faced me.

"Are you Jaxson Palmer?" he asked.

Dear God, please don't tell me Mrs. Ryan was behind this.

"Yes, why?"

"You have an early dismissal. Your parents are in the office, waiting for you," he said with a smile, and then walked away. What? Of all the years I'd been with them they had rarely ever picked me up from school at all, so an early dismissal was a complete shock. Still in disbelief, I made my way to my locker, packed my books, grabbed my jacket, and headed for the office.

Mark leaned against the front desk while chatting with the lady there. Natural laughter escaped Mark's mouth. That was hard to believe. It was just last night when I'd found out he was capable of smiling.

"Did something happen to Julia?" I asked.

"No. She's in the car. We're going to go out for dinner tonight."

Aliens. Yes – aliens had abducted them. Either that or they were under some form of hypnosis. I was willing to believe anything besides them actually making a change. I was silent throughout most of the car ride, trying to figure out what was going on. We hadn't gone out to eat in God knew how long. An apology. Maybe this was their way of apologizing for forgetting my birthday. Mark shifted the gears. This put a spotlight on the shirt he wore. I was so used to him walking around the house in beaten-up clothes, alcohol, and messy hair, and I'd never actually seen him when he tried to look presentable. There was even a struggle when it came to recognizing him.

He had on a white button-up, jeans, and, for once, he'd shaved. This was all too much to believe. The lady at the front desk had even smiled and waved to him on the way out. I bet she wouldn't have done that if she knew even a third of what life with him was like. The car ride was very silent until Julia broke it. "Jaxson," she said. Our eyes met through the interior window. We looked at each other momentarily before she finished her statement.

"How was school today?" she asked. Believe it or not, this was the first time she'd asked me that since my first day of freshman year.

Those days she showed more affection towards me, whether it was through secret movie days where we snuck off to the theater or when she would even protect me from Mark. Now that woman was nowhere to be found. Always standing by Mark, whether he was right or wrong. Wasn't alive with him but couldn't live without him. "It was just another day," I responded. She looked in the mirror and she smiled at me. Though my feelings towards her had changed drastically, I'll admit it was nice to see that smile again. I lowered my window and let the wind run over my face and through my hair.

About half an hour later we pulled over at a steakhouse. Mark walked around and held the door for Julia whilst I got out. We followed Mark inside. The wait was about 10 minutes before a waitress turned up. We were fairly quiet as we stared at our menus. Julia was the one to step up and break the awkward silence yet again. She and Mark began to talk about work. I had to be in some type of parallel dimension. A sound interrupted my thought process. Again it was the sound of laughter escaping Mark. And it wasn't the type he let out when messing around with his drunk buddies or his late-night sitcoms. A smart comment from Julia's mouth triggered it. Truthfully, it was nice to hear. I even found myself wanting to join in on their conversation now and then. By the time the waiter came around, I was the only one who knew what to order. "A grilled chicken sandwich," I answered. Julia ordered some type of fancy parmesan-crusted chicken meal she read from the menu and Mark settled on, "A good old-fashioned steak." And shortly after that, the two went right back to talking.

The delicious scent of meat wafted through the air. It was a far cry from the standard lunchroom indeed. *THUD!* The sound emerged from the right of me. Looking over, I discovered a family of four. The mother and father on one side of the booth, while their two sons sat across from them. The younger one had spilled his chocolate milk while the older one tried to clean it up. I watched them as the faces and table changed right before my eyes. Shifting and reshaping into a more familiar setting.

"*JAXSON, not again,*" *she sighed from embarrassment.*

Relax; it's only water, Jessica," said a man with chocolate brown skin and his famed cheesy grin.

"Yeah Mom, he's basically cleaning the table for us," laughed Noah.

"When your father and I told you to start thinking outside the box this is not what we meant," she replied. We all laughed over this statement for a bit. The light reflected off of her sterling silver necklace.

The younger me thought it was some bird. The older I grew, the more I realized it was a phoenix. I hadn't seen it nor her since that one night. But one thing I do remember is that she never took it off. Mom was a beautiful lady. She was always smiling, no matter how her day went. This world truly is a cruel one. "Jaxson, are you okay?" The voice. That warm, loving voice. The one that sang me to sleep every night. The loving voice that praised me every time I got an A on a spelling test. It was impossible but it was her. It was my mom. My head shot up quickly, but there was only disappointment. It was Julia, glaring at me with concern. I could feel water boiling in my eyes. "I need to use the bathroom."

I rushed to the bathroom, splashed some water on my face, and stared into the mirror. Some of the water had landed in my hair, causing it to hang over my forehead. I hated it when my emotions get the best of me. Through the mirror, I could see the window behind me. I turned around to face the opportunity. I could just leave right now. This life could be over with right now; all of it. My attention returned back to my caramel skin tone and dark brown eyes. If now was only the time. After splashing a couple more handfuls of water on my face I headed back to the table, and sat in silence for the remainder of our time there. I could be a lot of different people and I could feel a lot of different ways. But most of the time I'm just a boy who misses how things used to be.

Chapter 6

We both stood there. The silence between us louder than every passerby in the busy hallway behind us. My dry mouth opened to speak. "Hey look; the other day I didn't mean for any of that stuff to happen. I was just worried about you." She opened her mouth. Unsure of what to say she closed it, looked down, and shut her eyes. Her warm hand grabbed mine and she stepped forward, resting her forehead on my chin. "No…it's my fault for overacting," she said. I'm not too sure how she got them or who gave them to her, but I know her. And I also know she didn't deserve it. I moved my chin back and planted my lips upon her forehead.

"I don't know what's going on, but I'm here for you. Whether you want to tell me what's going on or not doesn't matter. Just know that I'm here." These were my words, which I whispered into her ear. Not only were these words fitting for the moment, they arose from a genuine place. She needed me. I needed her. "While we're here," I started, "there's something I've been meaning to ask you."

She backed up, preparing for what I was about to say. It didn't take a genius to figure out what I was about to ask her. And by the way her soft, pink lips puckered into a curved smile, I was confident she knew what was coming. "Victoria Alice Summers." As I said, this she never broke away from my eyes. This might have made others uncomfortable.

For me, it helped alleviate some of the stress from my system. My hand found its way to her cheek, "I was hoping you wouldn't mind going out with me."

"As?" she exaggerated the response, twisting her body slightly back and forth. I looked down and we both laughed for a bit.

"I'm sorry... I've never really-"

She interrupted me with a kiss on my lips. I could taste her strawberry lipstick; the last thing I wanted was for this moment to end. Releasing her was painful, to say the least. Clapping flowed through the air around us. It was from Jimmy and Angela. The words, "Damn it," came from Angela's mouth, while Jimmy held his hand out as if he was awaiting something. "You know, Vicky, I thought you could last another week or two," said Angela as she pulled a five-dollar bill out and reluctantly dropped it in Jimmy's hand. He then proceeded to put it to her eyes and pull it out. "No way. Jaxson here learns from the best. I told you the two would barely last a month," he shook his head back and forth proudly. After a few seconds, the dots began to click in my head. I was guessing Victoria realized it too by the way she dug her head into my chest and stated, "There's no way you two betted on us."

"Well. I would describe it as more of a wager," Angela reasoned.

I embraced Victoria in my arms.

"You know what? I'm okay with how this turned out." We hung around with Jimmy and Angela for a little while longer before we went our separate ways. Once

Victoria retrieved her books from her locker, we left the building and headed for an ice-cream shop.

"So have you been writing recently?" I asked.

She kicked a few pebbles out of her way before answering; I noticed this was something she did quite a lot.

"Yea," she responded.

"What do you write exactly?"

"Lots of short stories really, a couple of poems here and there," she said. "I read a lot more than I write."

"Stories huh? What genre?"

"Normally fantasy, those types of things always interest me. But a good amount of mystery and young adult slip in."

"Have you ever thought about going all the way and making a novel?"

She slowed down briefly and thought hard about the question.

"I've tried, but I can never finish them."

"Why not?"

"They're not that good"

"I bet they aren't," I responded.

She stopped walking and gawked at me.

I grabbed her hand and intertwined our fingers, "I bet they're great."

She smiled and rested her head upon my shoulders.

Julia, who hasn't seen a single report card of mine, stopped me with a question the moment I came through the door. "Do you have any homework to do today?"

"Yeah, only a bit," I replied, watching her wash off the kitchen countertop.

"That's good to hear," she said. "Mark's been waiting on you to get home for a while now. He has some kind of project for the two of you to work on." Her statement caught me off guard. A project. Before I would've completely ignored her comment, and a part of me still wanted to. Those steps and the thought of a nice shower accompanied by my mattress would top off an already amazing day. Still, with how strange they'd been acting lately, I was pretty curious. My feet traveled past her, dropping my book bag by the staircase, and towards the back.

Mark and I being alone together never lead to anything good. Hell, if I'm being honest, I don't even know the guy's middle name. My feet stopped in front of the garage door. My hand landed on the doorknob and pushed it open slightly, just enough for me to peek inside. He was working on what seemed to be an engine, even though there was no car in sight. The creaking of the door notified him that someone was entering. He stopped his tinkering momentarily. He looked tired and coughed a couple of times, which I presumed to be because of the dust. "You know, before I started working at a plant and making car parts, I used to be a street racer." He took a pause and looked up at me. No words left my mouth. He brushed dirt off his hands and sat down on top of a workbench.

"Yeah, Julia hated it. I was always out and she usually worried that I would get hurt or that I wasn't being faithful to her." He paused what he was doing and got a bit quieter. "I wasn't a saint then. Never have been, never will be. She's a good woman though." He stopped to scratch his head for a bit, "I don't deserve her." I kneeled down a bit. Embracing the sight of Mark taking responsibility for a mistake he made.

"Why don't you tell her this?" I questioned.

"Huh, perhaps I should," he said. Small talk with Mark generated an uneasy feeling. As odd as it was, I actually learned a thing or two about him. He met Julia in high school. They both were born in Rockwall. The two hadn't separated since. No matter how screwed up or blind they were, they never left each other's sides. Which I'll admit, is pretty impressive. I envy the bond they both share, which lead them over nine hundred miles away from home. Truly inseparable.

The rest of the night was pretty good. Julia made one of the best dinners she'd made in a long time and we all had a pretty good time conversing at the table. During the late hours of the night, the thought of why these two were acting like actual parents crossed my mind. I had no idea why, and as much as I thought about it, I realized I didn't care. It was nice to finally have it, after so many years of longing for it. I looked at my closet, which contained everything I needed for my great escape, and then I lay back and stared up at the ceiling. Maybe things could be different. Maybe things would be different. I closed my eyes. And that was when I heard it, -absolutely nothing. The peaceful night, wind, birds, and my thoughts were sound asleep. I could smile and mean it. Now lying on my side, I had a clear view of the night sky through my bedroom window. It pleased my eyes as I drifted off slowly.

Chapter 7

The TV screen laminated the dark room. Noah was in the kitchen making popcorn on babysitting duty. I flipped through the TV channels looking for some type of movie to watch. Click. Click. Click. I stopped abruptly. I was unsure, but I thought Mom and Dad's faces had flashed across the screen.

Moving back, I had to make sure. After a couple of clicks back, there they were again. Pictures of them across the big screen, side by side.

"Noah! Noah!" I ran down the hallway to the kitchen.

"Mom and Dad are on the TV!" I jumped in excitement.

"What?" questioned Noah, poking his head out from the kitchen.

"Come! Look!" I shouted, believing that they were now famous.

"Alright. Hold up a second." He began to make his way towards the living room.

"This better not be some kind of joke-" He stopped as soon as he saw the screen. His eyes were frozen in place.

"This is so cool right?" I asked, staring at him. In an instant, he dashed towards the phone.

"What's wrong?"

I turned back towards the screen. Now there was a picture of a tipped over car. I didn't pay any attention to the red one, because the only one that mattered was the dark blue SUV. The one which picked me up from school every day. It was theirs.

Gasping for breath, I came to life. The bed was drenched in sweat, my throat was desert dry, and I struggled to control my breathing. Why, why did I keep having the same dream over and over and over again? The thoughts raced through my mind as my fists slammed into my bedpost. I didn't think I'd ever be able to forget. My head lowered and as a few more tears escaped, I began to wipe them away. Marcus and Jessica Spencer were their names. The tragedy of the Spencer family was nothing more than just another article in the news, and that was what infuriated me the most because we were so much more than that. As usual, time passed, and we were all forgotten. And that's what happened. No relatives me and my brother could live with; no stable ones anyway. Compared to my brother, I received the short end of the stick when it came to being adopted.

I still remember when a couple in Ohio adopted him. Other kids were ecstatic for this opportunity. He received congratulations all night long. None of it mattered to him. He could no longer protect me anymore. Now he's off pursuing an engineering degree at Seattle University. Besides, the only thing I've envied of him is that he knew what he wanted to do and where he wanted to go in life. The alarm on my phone went off, buzzing against my dark brown nightstand.

It was just a way of letting me know that Mark was heading to work. Jimmy, Vicky, Angela, and I were planning to go to the movies later, around 3:00 pm, and since I didn't plan to go to sleep again I had a large gap of boredom to fill up. I started it off by heading to the bathroom to brush my teeth, wash my face, and fix my hair.

I made my way down to the kitchen, passing by the room both Mark and Julia shared. I took a peek inside and got a glimpse of Julia lying down, still asleep. She had another hour or so before she would head off to work. A growl rumbled in my stomach. Time for the most important part of the day. The sound of Julia getting up and walking into the bathroom emanated from the ceiling above me. Our floors were wooden, so it was pretty hard to miss. The expiration date on the milk was almost up, so I decided to at least get a couple more bowls of cereal in before we had to throw it out.

Knock! Knock! Knock! The sound came from the front door. Julia was still in the bathroom, so I took it upon myself to answer it. *Knock! Knock! Kno-* My opening of the door cut off the noise. A lady wearing a grey sweater who looked to be in her late twenties stood there. She had a white skin tone, short hair, and carried a clipboard among other papers in her hand. "Hi! How're you doing today?" she smiled. I'd never seen this woman before, so this whole encounter was a little odd for me.

"I'm doing fine. And you?"

"That's great to hear and I'm doing well, thanks for asking. Is Mark-" she stopped to take a look at her clipboard. "Is Mark Palmer here?" she asked, looking at me.

"Ummm…not at the moment, no. I'm sorry; who are you exactly?"

"Oh yes, my name is Jessy, and I'm with NCCN. We haven't been able to reach Mark over the phone and he hasn't replied to our emails, so we decided to see him in person."

"NCCN?"

Her eyebrows furrowed a bit, "National Comprehensive Cancer Network."

My entire body froze in place. All of the words that further came out from between her teeth went right over my head. "We're here because he hasn't been returning our calls. His test results came back and we believe his cancer is in stage four."

Cancer

Stage

Four

My body digested the words roughly. It seemed like all those years of drinking had finally caught up to him. Quite ironic how it had started when he was at least trying to get his act together. *Wait.* His act. Is that why all of a sudden he was making some major shifts in his behavior? It took cancer to open his eyes? I took her card and closed the door on her. My hand sat on it, as I was too busy thinking to take it off. The creaks from the staircase finally became loud enough for me to notice them over my thoughts.

"Jaxson, who was it?" Julia asked me. Her voice reminded me of a time when she'd cared. Which didn't at all help calm my shaking hand. I turned around, and threw the card on the floor beneath her. She stared at me, mouth hanging open, and then reached down and picked it up. Her hair was dripping wet and stuck together, courtesy of the shower she'd just finished. She placed her palm on her forehead, began to dig her fingers in, and then slowly dragged them down.

"Look Jaxson, I know-"

"It took this?" I shot my hand out and pointed at the card.

"It took this to make both of you care? So what, you guys thought you would come around, pick me up from school, go to some big restaurant and this would all be fixed?"

"Look; there are just some things you don't understand. And I'm sorry."

"What the hell is that supposed to mean?"

"Don't use that kind of language. We still-"

"Oh don't even pull that card. Don't you dare pull the parent card." I made my way past her. There were no words for me left to say.

"Jaxson, look, we're sorry. There are just some things that you don't know."

She said this as soon as I reached my room door. My blood was boiling.

"You know you keep saying that, but what does it mean?" My attention shifted towards her in search of an answer. "What does it mean?" She said nothing, only held her hand over her mouth. "Like I thought."

The door slammed behind me and I made sure to lock it. An impulse of rage overtook me at just the mere thought of them. And here I'd thought they cared about me for once in their lives. I was a fool to think people like them would change. My attention shifted to my closet.

Out of frustration my feet traveled there as fast as they could, my hands threw the door open; my mind had been wondering what it was like 1,000 miles from here, and I was ready to find out. This time I pried open the piece of the floor using my nails instead of a screwdriver. I grabbed as many outfits as I could and began to lay them over my bed. Today was the day for sure. No more constant bickering and no more of their irritating pettiness.

My hand was halfway through packing my first set of clothes when a loud ding mixed with a vibration rang across my room. I had forgotten all about that thing. I didn't have the energy or the motivation to go over to my bed and get it. But I knew who the text was from. It was from Victoria. I don't know what kind of trance she had me under, but it was enough to remind me of what I had here. And maybe she was saving me, because deep down, I knew I didn't have what it took to carry this thing off. Talking to her would help get my mind off of everything, even if it was just through a screen. My fingers turned on the screen and slid down to my messages.

The text said *Good Morning* with the sun emoji. She was always positive in the morning. Right now I couldn't match her mood. A second one appeared,

I'm excited to see you later ;)

She was the only person I knew of who still used semicolons and parentheses instead of just the normal smiley face emoji. I don't know what it was about that simple thing, but it made her text all the cuter. My back fell against the wall. A few minutes ago the pros of leaving outweighed the cons heavily in my mind. And now that I was calm, I could think clearly. If I ran, the only place I could go was to my brother who was about 2,000 miles away. The plan wasn't sufficient. It left me with one option: to stick around.

Chapter 8

As the day passed, three o'clock only crept closer and closer. The thought of canceling grew more and more tempting. I didn't know if I could make it through this movie or not. Still, the tickets were already paid for, and I didn't want to disappoint Victoria. She'd been talking about the movie ever since we'd formed the idea. The clock read 2:30, the movie started at 3:20, and Jimmy planned to have everyone picked up by 3:00. After a shower, finally eating breakfast, and working out a bit to relieve some stress, I'll admit I felt slightly better. Most of the rage had passed through my system; now there was sorrow. There was a sadness forming in my gut. One that appeared at the thought of actually losing Mark. I didn't want any of my friends to see me this way. Telling them was not a good idea. I knew it would change the way they acted around me. The trip they'd anticipated would now be a pity party for me.

Her simply being herself was enough to make me happy. Standing by the door with my back planted against the wall, I waited for Jimmy to arrive. Mentally preparing the facade that was about to be forced upon my face when I received a text on my phone. Jimmy claimed he was right around the corner. Knowing him, those words could mean he was miles away. Stepping out, I spotted Jimmy cruising down the block at once. Maybe miracles did happen, because the guy was on time for once. I looked up at the sky for the few seconds I had before he officially arrived. The sun was there; maybe if there wasn't a blanket of clouds covering it, I could've caught a glimpse. I walked across the cracked pavement and made my way to the street.

When I got inside the car, I closed the door behind me. I fixed myself on the polyester interior, let my head hit the back of my seat, closed my eyes, and took a deep breath. It only took a split second for me to accept that my whole "faking a smile" plan was going out the window. On the bright side, the fragrance inside this car was pretty nice. I had to hand it to Jimmy - if there was one thing he could do, it was keep a clean car.

"You okay?" he questioned with actual concern, which was rare for Jimmy.

"I'm fine, just a long night buddy. So, who're we going to get first?" I asked.

"They're both waiting at Angela's house," he said as he began to pull off.

"Well, isn't that convenient?"

The first few blocks were filled with a silence which I heavily appreciated due to the slight migraine forming in my head.

"Are you ready for the season to start?" Jimmy said, disrupting my sweet silence.

This caught me off guard, especially since it had been his idea to take a short break of a month or two. He claimed he had some "things to sort out." Knowing him, that could mean anything.

"What happened to having a slow start this season?" I asked, which out loud sounded worse than I thought it did in my head.

"That was before Brown and Davis got suspended. Coach needs people to fill in."

He stopped talking momentarily and took his eyes off the road to look over at me.

"We both know the rest of the guys aren't good enough, and you know how Carson gets when competition time begins to roll around."

"And since when do you, let alone anyone, care what Carson Daniels thinks?" I questioned.

"Never; I just want our team to do good. It is our last season after all."

As much as I hated admitting it, Jimmy was right. Of all our teammates on our boxing team, Carson was my least favorite. He was too loud, too impulsive, and beyond annoying. Just the thought of having to deal with him for even a moment enhanced my headache. It felt as if something was pounding against my skull. The discomfort consumed my mind so much that I hadn't even noticed our arrival at Angela's house.

Although two girls stepped out of the two-story, desert-tanned house, I only saw one. She wore a pink shirt with shoes that matched, and a pair of fitted jeans. If only I could slow down time to admire how gracefully she walked down the steps and towards the car. She smiled that wonderful smile. There it was again, the sun. It always shone down on her. It was as if it followed wherever she, and she alone, went. I didn't know what it was, but I couldn't get enough.

"You know what, I think I'm just going to get in the back," I said, patting Jim on the shoulder without even turning to look at him. I stepped out and left the door open for Angela to get in. I took a step to the right and held the backseat door open for Victoria.

I looked her up and down as she approached the door and then I opened my mouth,

"You look great."

"Thanks," she said, nearing the car as she looked down with a smile.

"But this is pretty basic," she said, while curling her hair behind her ear.

"Well, your basic could be someone else's amazing," I replied.

She smiled at this and kissed me on the cheek as she sat down in the car and moved two seats over. I glanced at Jimmy and Angela who were both nodding their heads in unison, looking at me through the side-view mirrors. Hiding my laugh, I climbed into the car myself. Angela and Jimmy began to engage in a conversation about some robbery that happened to a convenience store a couple of days ago, but I was too distracted to care. I looked over at her. My own painkiller. And she didn't even know it. My hand inched toward hers. When they met, she turned around and smiled at me as our fingers intertwined. As long as I was next to her I'd be just fine.

***

"You've got to be kidding me." As much as I hated it, as inconvenient as it was, there he was: Carson Daniels. He was a bit taller than me, with brown eyes and messy black hair. He was at the front of the line to the left of us. He and his two other friends were with him, disrupting the silence with their obnoxious laughter as usual. The mere sight of him was enough to add on to the aching sensation in my head. See, Carson didn't need any reason to start trouble; being himself was valid enough. I clenched Victoria's hand a little bit tighter as we moved a bit upward in the line. I began to occasionally glance over at Carson to see if he had noticed us. Around the 3rd or 4th glance I caught him staring right back at us. "Hey, would you do me a favor?" I faced Victoria.

"Can you go and find our seats? We're going to be in this line for a bit longer for the snacks, and I'm kind of bad with movie theaters," I stated in a convincing tone. "I'll go with her," said Angela immediately, and she grabbed her hand and dragged her off. I knew she would follow; those two were like a package deal at times. Taking a step forward, I informed Jimmy that Carson had seen us. It was only a matter of time before he made his way over here. It was actually a much shorter time than I'd thought it would be. He whispered something to his two followers and they stayed in line as he walked towards us.

"So, I haven't been seeing you boys at practice lately. Is there a reason why?"

As much as I wanted to give an immature response, I didn't have the energy to argue.

"Why do you care?" I questioned.

"Competitions are coming around and we're down a couple guys due to some... unfortunate events."

"And?" I asked. It was then that I realized that Jimmy had been unbelievably quiet throughout this entire exchange. This was very weird, considering that loud mouth he was known for.

"And, that means you need to get your shit together and come to practice," he said as he took a step forward. This was strike number one; now all I needed was two more.

"Take a step back," I said. He laughed at my response. My hands began to shake. Upsetting me was Carson's specialty. "What're you going to do?" he said with a sly smile.

But I didn't see him anymore; I saw Mark.

"*Were you drawing again?*" *he blurted, snatching the paper out of my hands. I had spent hours working on a picture of my old family.*

"*What'd I tell you about this?*" *he spat out as he ripped the paper in half.*

My eyes watered and tears began to stream down my cheeks as I looked up at him, dirty blonde hair and a wrinkled chin.

"*NOOO,*" *I rushed towards him, reaching for it.*

He held out his hand, clutched my shirt, and threw me on the ground. I felt the impact of my back colliding against the floor. He planted his foot on top of my chest and held me there. His cold, relentless eyes locked into mine.

"*You're wasting your time.*"

"This," he held my hard work up for me to see, and then tore it apart some more, dropping it to the floor afterwards, "it won't get you anywhere."

He took another step towards me. I heard nothing nor did I feel anything when I lunged towards him. At this moment my rage wasn't even for Carson's smug face - it was all for Mark.

"Jaxson, wait," Jimmy grabbed me from behind and we both fell backwards. I tried to fight my way out of it. When I looked up, there he was again. It was Mark, back in my room. He didn't say anything; he was just staring down at me in disgust with those steel eyes.

"WHAT DO YOU WANT?!" I screamed. I rushed to my feet, but Jimmy held me down tighter.

"Jaxson, Jaxson, chill bro. Look around you."

And somehow, I wasn't in my room anymore, I was in the theater lobby again. People scattered across the room stared at me. "Look man, just go to our seats. I'll get the snacks and take care of Carson," he said, putting the ticket in my hand "We're in theater 3C."

Everyone in the room was staring at us; more particularly at me. The jingle of keys could be heard coming from behind us. Two tall security guards with bulky builds jogged towards us. Slowing down their pace about ten feet away.

"What's going on here?" His deep voice overpowered every other sound in the lobby.

"Nothing at all, Sir," Carson said, while raising his hands in the air.

"You two, get up!" he shot at me and Jimmy, still on the floor.

"If any of you cause any more disruptions you're out!"

"Okay. Jeez, we're going," Jimmy responded, pulling both of us to our feet. I stared at Carson a bit more before I faced Jimmy. I decided to just listen to him and make my way downstairs to the theater rooms. Too pissed to acknowledge everyone staring at me, I stormed past them all. Walking down the hall gave me ample time to replay the events in my head. The thought of Mark's hands ripping up any art I made replayed itself over in my head.

Opening the door, I found Victoria waiting for me. She leaned against the wall with her arms crossed. Her facial expression instantly dropped when she saw my face. She continuously asked me what was wrong. I looked up and didn't tell her about Carson, or about what I'd discovered this morning. I told her about the stupid memory of Mark tearing up my drawing. Rarely do I ever expose my true emotions. The school counselor has been trying for five years to get me to open up and has never succeeded. But with her I felt so safe. So secure. After everything he'd done and the countless nights of agony he'd put me through, how could this be possible? I saw him in my head. The very thing that fueled me the most while I was on the punching bag. It's like he'd had a total transformation into someone I didn't even recognize. Cancer destroys, it doesn't fix. So how was it the cure to his disease?

Chapter 9

Stepping out of the dim movie theater was a fresh breath of air. An hour and 40 minutes and I had no memory of what the film was about. The only of us who had actually watched the film was Angela. Vicky lay beside me throughout the majority of the film, which I appreciated but which made me feel like a burden. And Jimmy didn't show up until 30 minutes into the film, without any snacks. He barely talked to anyone when he came back, and I was too busy dealing with my emotions to wonder why at the time. The soft touch of who I presumed to be Victoria landed on my hand and caused me to turn around.

"Let's go back to the lake," she said. "Last time we were there, I didn't get to show you what I wanted to. Now, I think you need it more than ever." And there it was; I had no idea what I was getting myself into, but as long as she was there it didn't matter. She had me under some sort of spell. And I had no intention of fighting it. "I'll ask Jimmy to take us," I said, gripping her hand a bit before letting go. "Give me a few, I'll be right back."

Straying away from her a bit, I was about to ask Angela where he had wandered off to when I found him standing next to a steel water fountain. "Jim." I approached him, attempting to capture his attention. He immediately shoved his phone inside his pocket and looked up frantically. "What!" he blurted out. His face was more anxious than angry. I looked at him with shock, "Jeez, what's got you so jumpy?" He rubbed his hand down his face before going, "Look, my bad bro, I've just got some stuff going on. What can I do to make it up to you?" "Well," I started, "we were just about to ask for a ride."

Shabbona Lake; last time we were here it didn't end that well, hopefully this time would be different. Stepping out of the car, I held the door open for her to scoot over and exit. Before we walked off, I rested my elbows on the passenger seat window in the front of the car. The metal stung my arms but I was already in this position and didn't feel like moving again. I asked Jimmy if he was okay, because he wasn't acting like the regular Jimmy Delgado I knew. After reassuring me that he was fine, I moved back and waved the two off. I definitely didn't believe him; however, I understood that some things just needed time to pass, so I let it go.

Turning around I was met with an exuberant Victoria, who stood in anticipation at the park's entrance. The gates were black and thin, shaping out a rectangular formation. The crunch of gravel beneath my feet notified her of my approach. She looked over at me and then returned her gaze as I got closer. "Follow me," she said before taking off into the park, laughing along the way. And purely out of instinct, not a thought in my mind, I took off after her. No clue where she was going, nor did I care. The magnetic force she carried wouldn't allow me to be too far away from her.

Her light brown hair fluttered wildly in the wind. I knew girls who never ran in gym class, let alone of their own free will. Unlike them, she enjoyed it. Holding her hands out, she looked as if she was about to hug the sky. We ran through the grass, over the hill, and down to the docks. I wasn't going to stop until she did. And she didn't stop until she met the railings, and even then she still crashed into them a bit. Catching up to her, I slowed down a bit. She was catching her breath and holding both hands on the rusted steel railing. The wind was weak as it breezed by her. And yet again, as if she hadn't just caught the attention of every bystander taking a casual stroll, her eyes were glued to the sky.

She turned back to me and said, "Come here," extending a hand for me. The dusky sun's sky reflected off the lake. What I saw was almost too perfect to believe. It looked like something straight out of some romantic movie. Nevertheless, I wasn't delusional. This was all real. Stepping forward, I reached out to accept her invitation. And when we met, it felt nothing like two oblivious teenagers goofing around on a dock. For the first time in a long time I felt that I had a reason to be here, even if it was temporary.

"When you told me what happened between you and your father, it got me thinking," she started. "I haven't told you that much about me. Jaxson, my home life isn't that great either. That's why I'm always hanging around after school. I hate going home," she continued. "Ever since my mom left us, I've been nothing but a reminder of her to my dad. I look so much like her." She looked over at me and said, "That's probably why he hates me so much." I didn't understand how she could say this and stand so freely. There wasn't a hint of sadness on her face; if anything there was just pure curiosity as she stared at the view in front of her. "We live in a trailer. My older brother moved out and my two younger siblings left with my mom. It's just me and him. Every day I hope she'll pop out of nowhere to come and get me. Well, that dream ran dry a long time ago."

"We're not that different, you and I. I guess that's another thing I like about you." She laughed a bit, looked down, bit her lip, and looked back up. "Before, it would bother me all day and night. Now it's not as bad."

"What changed?" I was curious about what she had discovered that had led her to forget something that painful. Needless to say, I was in dire need of the same thing. She slid to the left a bit towards me, and pointed out a finger that led straight into the horizon. "There's a place out there. I'm not sure what it's called, where it is, or its name. It's over the hill, past the lake, through the forest, and under the stars." Victoria Alice Summers. Turning to my side, I moved my right hand to her hip and the other gently onto her cheek. Taking in all of her beauty in this flawless moment. She had that look in her eyes. Sometimes I wished I could see the world through her eyes. I bet they traveled down the horizon and dove into the secrets it held.

"It's a place where the sun always shines."

Chapter 10:

I slightly choked while trying to chug down another bottle, leaving some to stain my white tank top. Lord knows I hated the taste, but I'd do anything to keep the thoughts from sinking in. *Cancer.* It had to be a mistake. No, it was a mistake. I'm not sick at all. I feel fine. "Yeah, just a mistake," I drunkenly mumbled to myself. It was the middle of the night and I struggled to make my way up the stairs. The creaks were extremely loud, and they seemed to only get louder every step I took.

On one step I didn't raise my foot enough and tripped up the stairs. I barely managed to stop my head from hitting the steps, but that came at the expense of the bottle falling out of my hands and spilling all over the steps. I took a deep breath, watching it fall.

Julia or the boy could just clean it up when the morning came. I pushed myself up and just as I made it to my feet, my foot slipped on a bit of beer that I hadn't noticed. Like a ball bouncing down a flight of stairs, I stumbled down and landed in a small puddle of beer that had escaped the bottle. Groaning in pain, I looked up at the pitch blackness surrounding me, too weak to move and too tired to try. The room spun around and my stomach was on the verge of pushing all of the liquid back out. Closing my eyes, I couldn't help it as the past began to mentally consume me.

Her wrinkled hand its way to me from the hospital bed, slowly but steadily. "Mark-" her voice was cut off by a few raspy coughs. I jolted up carefully, making sure not to rock her bed in the slightest, and grabbed her hand softly. "It's me, Mama," I said. My voice cracked and I choked back my tears. Seeing her like this was dreadful. Her blonde hair, which once shined as bright as the sun, had faded to grey. Her skin was filled with wrinkles and black spots, but I didn't care. She was still the same beautiful woman who had given me everything. She was still the woman who had stayed with me after my coward father left, she was still the woman who had got me ready for my first date, and she was still the one who had worked her ass off so I could go to school. She was still my mother. "Oh God, not like this, please not like this," I mumbled to myself, rocking back and forth softly in my chair.

The doctor had informed me to prepare my goodbyes because she didn't have much time left. That was a week ago. I looked up at her, and she was still smiling at me. That same smile she had when I finished my first baseball game and the same one she had when I got my driver's license. She'd been there for me whenever I needed it. And now look at her - she was lying on her deathbed and there wasn't a thing I could do to prevent it. Her breathing had slowed down and grown more irregular compared to what it was an hour ago when I'd arrived. I tried to ignore it as much as I could. Her breaths were becoming more and more short while the pauses in between grew longer. She took a deep breath as she gathered the strength to speak, and lifted her left hand up to my cheek.

"Oh, baby-" she managed to get out before having to take another breath, "Please don't-" she coughed a bit, "cry." She looked up at me; she was barely breathing anymore, yet she was still smiling as wide as she could. I heard one last raspy breath and she looked at me, as her eyes went stale and her hand dropped. The vital signs monitor to the right of me began to beep excessively loud. "No. No NO," I yelled as I jumped out of my seat. That sound. That sound. WHAT DOES IT MEAN?! My voice, growing angrier as more people flooded into the room. She couldn't be gone. There was no way. Right? Maybe it was- no, no way. She had time left and I was sure of it. "DO SOMETHING!" I yelled as a doctor and more nurses flooded into the room. "DON'T LET THIS HAPPEN!!" I shouted as I began to pull my hair in frustration.

Some security guards began to pull me out of the room, ignoring how much I resisted them. As I fought them away, one grabbed my legs while two others were restraining both of my arms. Staring at my mother in agony as they lifted me up and pulled me away, I saw the doctors plant their defibrillators on her lifeless body. No matter what the doctors or nurses said to me as my knees fell to the ground, all I heard was the sound of her flatline. That's all there was, that sound. I sat there as it played in my head over and over and over again.

As much as I didn't want to, I began to swallow the truth. She was gone. I had lost her. The click of footsteps began to echo through the hall. The footsteps slowed as he drew closer until eventually, he came to a stop. "She wanted me to give you this when it was her time." He handed me an envelope. I took it. He placed a hand on my shoulder, "Son, I've met a lot of people over the years. But none like your mother. I've never seen a woman so bright in such a predicament." As he talked, I stared down at the envelope. It was white with a red seal. I *clinched it tightly because this was all I had left of her. I looked up at him and back down at the letter. As he talked, I stared down at the envelope. It was white with a red seal. This was all I had left of her. Mom, I never even told you. It's Julia. I clinched the envelope tighter. She's pregnant.*

Wherever The Road Takes Us

Part 2

Chapter 11

"Speed..... I am Speed," A few moments of silence passed. "Yeah, this isn't going to work." A drop of sweat trickled down and through my eyebrow. We were on an early morning run. Our first boxing competition that we were actually going to attend was about a week away, and boy were we out of shape.

"It's probably because you don't believe in yourself," Jimmy responded.

I swear there was no way this guy was being serious half of the time. "Or maybe, just maybe, it's because you've been telling me to repeat the same quote from the Disney movie *Cars* for the last two days for no reason." A moment of silence passed.

"You know, I really did think a lot about what you just said. And I still think my answer makes more sense," he replied.

I palmed my face. Jimmy Delgado was one helluva guy. As sarcastic and mind-boggling as a lot of things he said might be, I wouldn't have anyone else as my closest friend. We'd been thick and thin together, and it'd been this way since the day we met.

"Jeez, what'd they do to you?" It was hard to understand the words over the sound of rain trampling against the alleyway ground. And it was even harder to look up due to my multiple injuries, but when I did, I saw some boy I'd never seen before. His face was littered with freckles and I could see a patch

of red hair stick out from underneath his yellow rain jacket. I gave no words as a response, due to the fact I had no energy for it. Even then, he still held out a hand to help me up.

I hesitated for a moment, trying to figure out why he would do this for someone he didn't even know. Normally I wouldn't trust people I'd never met; however, I was tired of being in that alleyway.

He helped me up and I wrapped my arm around him for a bit of extra support. I groaned as the pain in my stomach ached a bit while I rose up.

"How'd you even end up here? Like this?" he questioned.

"Muggers," I groaned.

In truth it wasn't a mugger at all; this was the work of Mark after my first attempt at defending myself. Jimmy took me home. And when his mom opened the door, her face was distraught. She instantly ran for the ice bags as Jimmy and I struggled to the couch.

That night was horrible at first, but now I wouldn't trade it for the world. That was the first time I'd had a home-cooked meal in a while. We jogged further down the sidewalk and began to pass Mr. Meeks house when Jimmy noticed the house and raced across the street with no hesitation. I couldn't believe it. "THERE'S NO WAY YOU'RE STILL SCARED OF MS. FLUFFLES!" I hollered across the street, cupping my hands over my lips. "SHE DIDN'T BITE YOU!" Jimmy yelled back. Yeah, well, that was pretty fair. Last year Jimmy and I were out, late at night, messing around in the alleyways. I guess Mr. Meeks forgot to chain up his dog because when we turned the corner, we found his Doberman sniffing around some trash. His dog had to have been at least ninety pounds at the time. That was one of the best nights of my life - it was the night Jimmy gained his fear of dogs.

We both stood there, frozen, as the beast stared at us and snarled.

"Why the hell would you poke it?" I questioned as silently as possible. "Why would you dare me to do it? You know Delgados never back down from a dare," he responded. I rolled my eyes.

"Okay, look," he said. I braced myself, because whenever he started a sentence with those two words it would always end horribly.

"We're going to have to jump it," he said.

"What?" I shouted as quietly as I could as my face shot towards him.

"We don't have many options," he replied.

The monster in front of us moved another paw forward.

Needless to say, she looked pissed. Her growl got louder, and she let out a menacing bark.

"On 3," he said. "1," he began the countdown and I clenched my fist.

"2," she lowered her body, preparing to pounce on us.

"3!" I was paralyzed with fear; meanwhile Jimmy turned around and shot down the alleyway in the opposite direction.

I'd never seen him run that fast, not even in practice. Turning around, I mentally calculated on a scale of one to ten how screwed I was. "You've gotta be fuc-" Ms. Fluffles interrupted my sentence by pouncing on my chest and knocking me on the ground. Afraid to open my eyes, I thought my time on this earth was over. And then, a miracle happened. She spent less than two seconds hovering over me before she jumped off of me and took off after Jimmy.

The best of it all being that she was much faster than him.

Jimmy Delgado truly was a piece of work. "I'm about to start heading home!" I shouted across the block. "You sure you don't want to come over? We could hit the punching bag for a bit!" he suggested.

"Tempting... Maybe later," I said. During my climb up the porch of my house, I kneeled down and picked up the newspaper. Taking off the rubber band wrapped around it, I was met with a title of, *"Another Robbery Strikes Sycamore!"* This was the fifth one this month. And I thought the worst thing that would ever happen here was when Jimmy and I used to kick over random trash cans in our freshman year. I stared at the door in front of me, dreading having to go inside.

If I wasn't doused in sweat and starving, maybe I could've turned around and run anywhere else. Opening the door, the scent of breakfast being prepared filled the air. The smell of pancakes and sausages made my stomach gurgle. It would be hard to ignore it today. Mark was sitting in his chair checking a small pile of mail. I'd felt his gaze since I opened the door. I didn't look at him, look his way, or acknowledge him at all. My eyes stayed glued to the stairs in front of me as I strolled past him. One step at a time, never looking back.

When I reached the top of the stairs, the atmosphere instantly shifted into that of a safe zone. I needed to focus on what mattered. I had a boxing match coming up and I was beyond unprepared. I started up the water for my shower, and during my wait I heard the ring of a notification from my phone. It was from Noah, but his name was still disguised under Benjamin. I picked up my phone and stared at it. The distance from Sycamore to Ohio was a six-hour-two-minute car ride, thirty-two-hour bike ride, and a one-hundred-thirteen-hour walk. At one point I was ready to try out just about any of them. Initially I was planning to finish my senior year before I left. Now, with the way things had been going lately, I just didn't know anymore. I stepped into the bathtub and immediately felt the pressure of the sparkling hot water shower down on me.

It was all so simple at one point, and I let that thought repeat itself over and over in my mind. Truthfully, I knew it wasn't everything that made it complicated. If I had known Mark was dying earlier, I would've tried to leave sooner. I reached for a soap bar. Although I loved Jimmy like a brother, I was even ready to leave him behind, as guilty as it made me feel. I laid my head back and stared at the ceiling. The problem was her - Victoria. A little piece of heaven that fell from nowhere and landed on my doorstep. I took a deep breath. She made me feel a way I didn't ever think would be possible if I stayed here. She gave me hope. Even though it was a small strand, it was enough to give me a run for my money.

My thoughts were interrupted after various text messages coming from my phone. It was probably just Jimmy sending some memes he'd found. When I finished showering, I stepped out to the fog of a bathroom, grabbed a towel and my phone, and proceeded to check my text messages. I was correct about my meme prediction. Scrolling down a bit further, there was one message I didn't expect. The message was sent from Victoria.

In the movies you told me what happened to you. And I believe that no talent should be wasted. So,
I decided to get you something. Be outside in 15 ;)

That was 10 minutes ago. Practically falling into my room, I dried off my body as fast as possible. Quickly searching through my clothes I settled on a black V-neck shirt, hoping it would show off some of my muscles. I stopped in front of the mirror, checking my face and hair to see if either was moisturized. *DING!* The sound came from the front door. No. I wanted to burst out of my room, open the door for her, and drag her far away from these two. I knew this was impossible now. Julia had opened the door, and her conversation with Victoria could be heard. I propped open my room door a bit in hopes of better hearing their conversation. So far it sounded like she had already brainwashed her; this had to be record timing.

It was a tough call, but I decided to make my appearance downstairs. Opening the door, I placed a hand on the banister and tried to get down the steps slowly without making a creak. That failed as three steps down I caught both of their attention. Even in this awkward predicament, I still couldn't take my eyes off of Victoria. Just like every other day, she looked amazing.

"Don't you think she should stay for breakfast too?" Julia smiled at me, "There's enough food for everyone." I looked at the two wide-eyed; they both stared back at me.

"Thanks Ms. Palmer, but it really isn't th-"

"Nonsense. You come on in," Julia insisted, opening the door wider while motioning for her enter.

CHAPTER 12

There were a lot of places I'd rather us be right now, the bottom of the Atlantic included. An awkward silence filled the air. We sat in the dining room. A wooden table separating us from each other. We only used this space when there was company, so basically never. I tapped on the table, just counting down the seconds passing. Studying the table as Julia began to lay out different plates, filled with breakfast, around the table. Maybe today was a special day I didn't know about because she'd made a huge breakfast filled with: scrambled eggs, waffles, Italian sausage, biscuits, and grits. Although I was annoyed, I'll admit it did look pretty delicious. Too bad they had probably poisoned it

***

Why did he look so upset? I stared across the table at Jaxson's curly black hair, brown eyes, and caramel skin. He'd barely even looked up at me or anyone this entire time. His mother motioned her arms out. "Don't be shy," she said, while holding the back of Mr. Palmer's chair. So these were his parents; it's funny because they look nothing alike. Jaxson's father, he wasn't as bad as I had pictured. In fact, he looked pretty nice and clean in a sense. His dad took no hesitation and went in for the sausages as his mom began to make her way around the table, towards her seat.

My eyes followed her a bit and stopped once she passed Jaxson. He looked over at his father in disgust, and then he took a glance at Julia as she sat down. Still, not a word escaped his mouth. I began to speak up, "This all looks great Mrs. Palmer." Right after this, my eyes took a quick shift towards Jaxson, fast enough for me to see him roll his eyes. Okay, now that was a little rude. "So," Julia started, as she picked up a bowl of grits and began to distribute some on each of our plates, "how'd you two meet?" Julia said with a beaming smile. I looked down a bit to hide the blush that was forming across my face.

"Ohh, I know that face," chuckled Mr. Palmer with some laughter behind it. Everyone had food on their plates. Well, almost everyone. As I began to talk more with them, I realized they weren't that bad. Mrs. Palmer had a smile that never left her face, and she reminded me a lot of my mom. Although it's been awhile, I still remembered every detail about her like it was yesterday. And Mr. Palmer was pretty funny. We had been talking for a while now and it still bothered me that Jaxson had yet to pick at his food or even say anything. In fact, it seemed as though he was only getting slightly angrier the more we laughed. I didn't get it. He had so much in front of him and it was like he didn't even care.

I noticed that in between our conversation, the two quieted down a bit and began to look at each other. They whispered to each other and they both glanced at Jaxson; I couldn't make out what they were saying. After one final nod, Mrs. Palmer reached across the table and rested her palm flat against the table, inches from Jaxson's.

"Jaxson," she started, "you had a long run this morning and I think you sh-"

"I'm not hungry," he said, cutting her off.

Her face sunk a little bit. His actions were starting to tilt me. His father spoke up. "Jaxson," he started, and in an instant his eyes flicked to his left and stared at him in the eyes. "Your mother has-"

"My mother?" Jaxson replied, cutting him off. He shot out of his seat so fast it actually shocked me. The table rocked. I stared at him filled with questions. Why was he so pissed? And why was he being so sarcastic about Mrs. Palmer being his mom?

"Jaxson, look," he started again.

No," he began to walk away.

He said nothing at all while he grabbed his jacket and rushed out of the door. Mr. Palmer dropped his utensils on his plate and then immediately began to rub his fingers back and forth over his forehead. Julia's eyes stayed on the door. The breakfast she'd created, and this was the thanks she got? I stood up and said, "You made a wonderful breakfast. I'd better go." I grabbed my hoodie, made my way to the door, and looked furiously around for him; needless to say I was pissed. I immediately spotted his grey Nike fleece jacket to my left. He was halfway down the block. "Jaxson," I said, lightly jogging to catch up.

"Hey!" I shouted loudly while grabbing his shoulders. He whipped around and looked at me. His eyes were burning. "What the hell was that?" I asked, throwing my arms out wide open.

"It was nothing," he said while shrugging his shoulders and looking off to the side.

"No, it was something," I said as I pointed back to his house "They made a great breakfast for you and they even invited me in."

"They did all of that for you to act like this!" I said, motioning my arms up and down his body toward him. He let out a small laugh and rolled his eyes a bit.

"So you think it's funny?"

"You don't even know," he responded. "You're just going to believe whatever little show they put on. That isn't them," he pointed down the street at his house. I put my head up towards the sky and shut my eyes. I remembered what he told me had happened between him and his dad. I brought my head back down and took a deep breath before I opened my eyes. "Look, I know they haven't always been the best parents, but what I saw in there showed that they were really trying. And they didn't deserve the reaction you gave to them."

Emotions poured out from me and I went on. I pointed towards my chest, "I wish I could come home to something like that, but I can't." My voice began to crack. My hands were shaking and my heart was pounding. "I'll call you later," were his final words before backing up, turning around, and then walking away. Out of frustration with him I pushed my hands into my pockets.

Chasing after him was the only move I wanted to make. Turning around, I concluded the best thing to do was leave it alone until we'd both calmed down. Well, this truly was one hell of a Sunday morning. Was it even morning? The clouds covering the sky around us definitely didn't make it feel that way.

***

Boom! Boom! Boom! I unloaded every bit of anger I could upon the bag. "Jeez man," Jimmy's head poked out from behind it. "What has the bag ever done to you?" Ignoring his comment I continued to punch the bag. The thought of the breakfast from earlier fired me up even more. How could she stand up for them?

Boom!

They really think one crumby,

Boom!, breakfast would make up for the years?

Boom!

Stupid Mark.

Boom!

Stupid Julia.

Boom!

BOOM!

"Okay, now you need to relax." Jimmy pulled the bag out of my reach. I took a moment to catch my breath. We were in his basement punching an old, black boxing bag, which hung from the ceiling and which now held a few more dents in it. The bag was one of the few things Jimmy's father had left behind. "Look, I appreciate the fact that you want to get some extra practice in," he said while beginning to take the gloves off of my hands "But I don't think just punching this bag will fix your problems." I struggled to unwrap my sore hands.

"You need to talk to them. All of them," he said. When I finally finished unwrapping them, I noticed how bright red they were. It was as if I'd held them over a stovetop. "Jim, I need you for a second," his mom shouted down their stairwell. "Well, duty calls," he said before heading up the stairs. Not only was Jimmy's basement the least creepiest one I've ever seen, it was also the coolest. Not only did he have his own private gym filled with weights and different types of workout equipment, there was also a 32-inch flat-screen TV, and a trophy shelf which I paused to take a closer look at. There were medals, ribbons, pictures, etc.

Jimmy's somewhat of a small-town celebrity. Analyzing the awards further, I spotted a news article on one shelf. Picking it up, there was a nice shot of some man delivering a hook across his opponent's face; you could see his spit flying in the air. The title read, "Delgado Takes Another Win!" I guess boxing really was in his blood. A sound coming from behind me interrupted my thoughts. It was a constant vibration and I predicted it to be Jimmy's cell phone. I located his phone by the weights in the far-left corner of the basement. I didn't care at first. Mainly because I presumed it to be Angela; however, the caller ID left me stunned - "Carson." Now, normally I wouldn't care if it was anybody else from wrestling, but I knew for a fact that Jimmy hated that guy as much as I did. Why did he even have his number stored? It was his business after all, so I brushed it off as nothing and let the call die out. I was a couple steps away before I heard the sound of a text message go off. It wasn't long before curiosity took over my legs and turned me back around.

It read:

321 State St, 7 PM, Sunday.

I didn't recognize the address, nor did I know what the purpose of this text was at all.

Another message came through. I just assumed it was some afterparty I hadn't caught wind of, considering that Sunday was a couple of days after our first match.

And don't be late this time.

This time? What was that supposed to mean? For some reason I couldn't rub off the feeling of needing to know what that meant. I heard Jimmy make his way down the steps, so I quietly rushed to my phone and jotted down the address, day, and time from pure memory. I planned to check it out later. For now I still hadn't figured out how I was going to make things right with Victoria. And I hated to admit it, but the things she'd said to me after breakfast - did she have a point?

CHAPTER 13

SMACK! The fist connected against the center of his cheek; Jimmy always did have a killer right hook. It was pretty obvious that Jimmy had got the guy good. He stumbled around the ring in his green uniform with golden trims. Jimmy noticing this and began to showboat a bit and raise his fist in the air as if the match was already over. The crowd began to cheer him on, as they always did. "Classic Jimmy," I lightly chuckled. "God damnit Delgado!" Coach exclaimed loudly, taking off his hat and waving it around trying to capture his attention. Under his wrinkled skin, agitated face, and baseball cap that covered most of his grey hair, I knew even he was delighted by the sight in front of him. Jimmy was arguably the best boxing prodigy Sycamore had ever seen. There were so many colleges giving him offers that we both lost count months ago.

That was one thing I always envied about Jimmy - he knew what he loved, and he would spend his life doing so. Jimmy shuffled towards the guy a bit with his guard up. I already knew what was coming up; "The Delgado Special." He ducked down and hit the guy twice in the stomach, and then he finished it off with one of his signature uppercuts. He actually knocked the mouth guard out of the guy's mouth this time, shooting his face up. "That's one of the moves his father taught him," said Mrs. Delgado, although she preferred that I called her Evalend. She spoke again, "I haven't seen it in a while." I looked over at her as she watched him gracefully with a warm, loving smile. Jimmy and his mother shared a powerful bond.

No matter how small the achievement or how far the travel, she was always there for him. There was no doubt about it that Jimmy was the best out of all of us, and there was no doubt that everyone knew it. As soon as his guy hit the ground, Jimmy started moon walking around the ring.

"Did his father teach him that?" "No," she laughed lightly, "that's all Jimmy." The referee called the fight - the winner was very clear. I checked the board; next was me. Evalend also noticed this and patted me on the back, "Go get him."

"Will do Ma'am,"

A pit of anxiety formed in my chest. Not just because of the fight, but because I didn't know if Victoria was out there or not. Jimmy informed me that she'd told Angela she would be here today. Scanning through the crown for a glimpse of her, I found nothing. Coach made sure my white and black gloves were strapped on and my headgear was on tight. I wished he would have gotten done with that sooner. The smell of his bubblegum breath covering the air around us agitated my nose. My opponent stepped into the ring; he was muscular, and I presumed he weighed a pound or two more than me. Our heights, however, were about the same. His eyes stared me down. At first it was intimidating, then it became pretty weird. "Get him, Rock!" I heard his teammates shout behind him. Of course the guy I matched against had some sort of nickname.

The ref spread his arms and motioned for the two of us to come in. He stepped forward first, anxious to start the fight. Once we were done touching gloves, we broke off back to our corners. I'll admit this guy looked menacing, but I bet I had a lot more anger reserved. *Ding!* The bell rang, signaling the beginning of the fight. We danced around a bit before he went for the first strike. I weaved his jab and shot him once in the stomach. After that I shot for two jabs to his face and dashed back afterwards. They both missed. I blocked a couple of his punches and ducked under his left hook. When I came back up, I landed a clean cross on his right cheek - the feel of landing this punch was beyond satisfying. I could hear my team roar behind me. Okay, now I just needed to land one more of those and I'd win the bet against the coach. He stumbled back and fixed himself back up. This time, he looked pissed. I nodded my head to the right and shrugged my shoulders slightly; this was my way of communicating to him that "shit happens."

He lost all of his form and sprinted towards me, getting back in his position when he reached me. He let off a fury of punches on me. I dodged most until one of his many wild hooks landed on my chin. Right after that, the bell rang. I backed up into my corner and sat down and he went back to his. Even though I could still feel the force of his punch still lingering on my face, he really didn't have much - compared to Mark, that was. One thing I can say he's done is teach me how to take a punch. Coach pulled the mouth guard out of my mouth while Jimmy poured some water in. "He's strong-" started Jimmy.

"But his form is wild," I said, cutting him off.

"He goes mostly for haymaker swings-" started Coach.

"And if I go for straight punches I'll get to him first."

"There we go," he said, slapping me on the shoulder and popping the mouth guard back in. I knew this type of fighter. He depended on knocking you as his main form of winning. Luckily enough I'd sparred against people like Carson enough to know how to handle this guy.

Ding! went to the bell, initiating the second round of the fight. We neared each other and I immediately went for a jab to his gut. He was fast enough to block this and there it was, another hook. I was ready this time, and while his arm was still swinging around horizontally, I struck him twice in the face. Shuffling forward, I clocked him with a right hook of my own. When his face rocked left, I hit him with an uppercut coming from my left hand. If strength was the only advantage he had, then it was going to be a bad fight for him.

Mid-fight the words, "MAXIN JAXSON!" erupted in the air like lightning. I instantly recognized the voice of Jimmy, who's infamously known for making up the worst nicknames known to mankind. Unfortunately, the entire audience didn't realize this, and began to follow in on his chant. Roars of "MAXIN JAXSON" filled the air. Literally any other name was better than that one. Deciding to talk about it later, I concentrated on the fight. Ducking under his next attack I twisted my entire body, exerting all of its force into an uppercut on his stomach with my right arm. I hate to sound cocky, but I really was faster and smarter than this guy. He fell down to his knee and the ref began his count. By the time the ref got to six he was back to his feet.

"Come on, Rock! Stop messing around with him," I heard come from the people behind him.

Determined to not lose in front of his team, he straightened himself back up. We probably had about 30 seconds left in this round and the next one would be our last. He threw out a jab, parrying away and I struck him in the face with the same hand. Immediately after that he answered back with a powerful haymaker that I hadn't anticipated, which landed directly on my cheekbone. Brushing it off I regained my posture and prepared for his next move. Focusing in I saw his next move before it happened. The twitch of his muscle, the way he leaned forward - it had to be a cross. I planned out the perfect account. When he went for it, I used the sweat in my shoulder to slip it off. I put everything inside of the left hook that came crashing against his skull. The backlash of the force brought pain to my wrist. The crowd went silent and then an ear-splitting combination of people screaming surrounded me when he hit the ground.

Looking into the stadium it felt amazing to hear people cheering me on, even if it was a horrible name. All types of different - wait. Was that-. Standing in the second row, two seats over were three very familiar faces. Mark, Julia, and Victoria. How did they find each other? How did they know? I had a lot of questions, but I didn't think any of them mattered at this moment. When they began to announce me the winner, I saw that Jimmy was introducing his mom to Julia, Mark, and Victoria.

The fact that the referee was holding my hand up in victory was fruitless - my eyes were still locked on the five people waiting for me to come down. I ended the gesture shortly and tossed the medal to Coach. He loved to hang them on the wall for display. Making my way down to ringside, Victoria's words found their way back to my head.

"Look, I know they haven't always been the best parents, but what I saw in there showed that they were really trying. And they didn't deserve the reaction you gave to them."

The words rang through my ears.

"I wish I could come home to something like that, BUT I CAN'T!"

As much as I hated admitting it, she had a point. I approached them and heard a lot of things. Jimmy grabbed my shoulder and said, "Yep folks, it's true."

He pushed it around a bit, "I taught him everything he knows."

Ms. Delgado stepped forward, retracting Jimmy into her arms, "Never mind him, Jaxson, you both did great today."

"No, you both did amazing," said Victoria. I was happy she was there. She stepped forward and planted a kiss on my cheek. I took that as a sign she wasn't upset with me anymore.

"That they did," Julia said, establishing both her and Mark's presence. She put both hands on my shoulders and stopped in front of me. She leaned in and did something that absolutely shocked me. She kissed my forehead, ignoring the sweat that dripped off down it. Skepticism that that had just happened poured into my mind. Even though it was hard to believe, I kind of liked it. She stepped back, and Mark stepped forward.

Nervously, he tried to form words. He started a few sentences that he was obviously unsure of before letting out a sigh. He extended his hand out. It was hard not to think about all he'd done. Taking Victoria's advice and trying to focus on what he was doing now would be a tough process. It may have seemed like a simple handshake to everyone else, but he and I knew it was much more than that. Unsure of what was to come next, my hand drew closer to his. One thing I did know was that Mark was running out of time. And no matter how much we tried to ignore it, it was coming. His hand met mine. Our story was far from a good one, but maybe, just maybe, the ending could be different.

Chapter 14

"Where did you get this?" A blazing red 2009 Dodge Challenger sat in front of me, its outdated red paint and black trimming clearly noticeable.

"I did tell you I was a street racer, remember?"

"Cynthia and I took a lot of cash home," he said, patting his hand on the hood.

"Where did you keep this?" I questioned. I'd been here for years and never seen this thing.

"I kept it in stora-" a couple of dry coughs escaping his throat cut him off. He blocked his mouth with his arm and when he was done, he finished his statement, "storage."

"She's been locked away for too many years," he continued. "How about we change that?"

"You want me to help you fix this car?"

"Mm-hmm," he grinned. Seeing him smile was about as rare as a bigfoot sighting. Part of me wanted to take a picture and upload it to the internet. It was hard to picture. Mark and I alone. In the garage. Working together on a car. I pinched my thigh to ensure this wasn't a dream. Before, I would've said no in a heartbeat. Now, maybe it wouldn't be such a bad idea.

"Quick question," I started, "what made you decide to do this?"

Walking around the car's front he unlocked the driver's door and put a foot inside, leaving his head and the other half of his body still outside. "I've been wanting to get her back on the road for quite some time now. A couple more nostalgic rides wouldn't hurt." He stopped in his tracks, "Well, that is, before I pass it on." He tossed the black keys over the car roof towards me. He caught me off guard, but my hands shot up just in time to catch them. I inspected the teardrop-shaped remote which had the word "DODGE" plated in silver on its back. "If you help me get her up and running, she's all yours. Consider it a late birthday gift."

"Well," I held the keys in my hand tightly and looked up, "you've got yourself a deal."

"Great; we'll start when you're home."

On my way to the door something caught my eye. There was a dent on the front passenger door. It was faint and barely noticeable. "Hey, what happened here?" I asked, pointing towards it. Weirdly enough, Mark said nothing at all as he stared at the door. "Mark?" I exclaimed, trying to capture his attention. "Mark!" I said again, this time clapping my hands. This woke him from whatever trance he was under. He was a bit quieter now, "That's just some incident I had." He turned around and picked up a wrench, "It was a long, long time ago."

Oh no, not her. Mrs. Ryan stood at the front of the lab talking to the current computer lab monitor. I'd only wanted to finish submitting some homework due tomorrow during free period. It was only supposed to be a five-minute job, but I knew if she saw me, I would be trapped for about another twenty minutes. After clicking submit, I ducked under one of the black monitors. She took a long survey of the room, taking her time going from left to right. I prepared my rush for the door when she started a stroll into my direction. I stepped back into my safety behind the monitor. She stopped by the printer. Once she got her papers and left, I'd be in the clear.

With a few extra moments to spare I decided to make use of my time. "321 W State St," was the address Jimmy was supposed to meet Carson at tonight. I mumbled it to myself a couple of times as I searched it into the web. Sycamore Antiques showed up across my screen. This was strange; why were they meeting up there? I'd expected a pizza parlor or gym of some sort. What the hell did any of us know about antiques? I made sure to check both ways before leaving the lab. The coast was clear. I was heading towards the stairs when I heard, "Jaxson Palmer." She'd found me. But how? "Or should I say Maxin Jaxson!" she laughed and pumped her fist in the air. The act was extremely cringey to watch. Fifty percent of the smile I gave her was genuine; the other was to make the conversation as brief as possible.

"I saw you out there the other day. You did great!"

"Thank you," I responded.

"I won't take up too much of your time, because I know you all are busy nowadays. How've you been feeling lately?" she questioned me.

"Honestly," I began while taking a step down the stairs, "I've been pretty damn good."

"Language!" I heard from behind me as I jogged down the stairs. It made me smirk as I headed for my locker. To my surprise, Victoria stood next to my locker.

She had on a long, grey, long-sleeve t-shirt. Accompanying her was a black beanie, which hung off the top of her head. It was different, yet cute. A blue paper bag sat on the ground beside her, spotted with white circles in all different shapes and sizes. I sped up towards her and put my hands on her waist as she held hers around my neck. "Why the hat?" I kissed her on the lips, and we began to rock left and right slightly.

"Trying out a new style," she paused. "You like it?" she questioned me. "I loveeee it," I replied in a flirty tone.

"What's in the bag?"

"Oh that? It's just the gift I never got to give you at the wonderful breakfast we had the other day," she answered sarcastically.

I separated from her a bit, remembering my behavior from the other morning.

"Listen I-"

"Shhhhh." She hushed my lips by placing a finger vertically over my lips.

"It's all water under the bridge. don't even think about it," she said with her signature smile. With a girl like her you didn't need any fireworks in the background or amazing scenery to complement it. Simply having her in my arms made this perfect.

Opening the package at home I uncovered a large notebook. It had a black cover and around a couple hundred pages within it. The sheets were wide and thick. I was confused about what this had to do with her text message saying that since she didn't believe dreams ever die that she'd decided to get me this. Then I remembered my old drawing hobby. Usually I received gifts that satisfied some temporary needs or even a useless accessory that I normally wouldn't mind. However, this book. It was very thoughtful of her. Underneath the book was a miniature painting kit, a pack of colored pencils, and a bunch of markers. A folded-up piece of paper lay off to the side.

Don't let the paint run dry.

I caressed the note with my thumb before laying it down and heading towards the door. How thoughtful of her. Based on the way things were going I might actually be able to put it to good use. When I finished sliding on a black hoodie, I fixed my hair in the mirror. The time was 6:30 and the antique store was about three or so miles from my house. I connected my headphones to my phone, slapped on a random playlist, and headed downstairs. Inches away from walking out of the door before I stopped myself. Usually I would leave with no explanation as to where I was going. I released the golden doorknob and stopped by the dining room. Both Julia and Mark were snuggled up on the oceanic Lawson couch, watching some old sitcom. I could hear their laughter whilst approaching the living room. I found it pleasurable to the ears. "Hey guys," I spoke up. They both turned around and looked my way. "I'm going to go out for a run; I should be back by dinner."

They looked at each other. This was clearly as new to them as it was to me. "Yeah that's fine," Mark spoke up. "Just be safe out there," he said. "Will do," I saluted him off and patted the wall next to me twice before my exit. My footsteps crashed into the tropical red sunlight reflecting over the puddles in the street. The dimming sun made me regret not leaving a bit sooner. A few minutes of seeing the sun would have sufficed. I've always had a thing for running. It's one of the few things that actually puts my mind at ease. Sprinting at my full speed with the wind rushing against my face and blasting a killer track felt great to me. It took away everything; every little problem and inconvenience didn't matter in moments like these. I loved them, I truly did.

The streetlights wouldn't be on for about another thirty minutes. It didn't matter anyway, I wasn't far from the store now. I ran down a side street filled with a collection of nice, two-story houses. I took this path not only to kill an extra couple of minutes, but to enjoy the pleasantness of this area. The houses were pretty similar, only different colors differentiating them. The cars were a different story. There was a pink Nissan, blue Prius, yellow Camaro, red truck- wait, I knew that truck. I crossed the street and slowed down as I began to pass it. The redness of my GMC and a license plate I instantly recognized.

Yep. It was definitely Jimmy's. But what the hell was it doing out here? I scanned my surroundings; the truck was empty and there was no one in sight. This was a bit confusing - I wanted to call him up right then and there but refrained from doing so. After some thought, I decided to finish making my way to the store. I was only about a block or so from the store, and instead of jogging around I decided to cut through a nearby alleyway. A couple steps in I made out two dark silhouettes standing in the alleyway. I ducked behind a nearby garbage can. Doing so, I unintentionally scraped my shoe against the brick wall. Their conversing stopped. I assumed that they were looking my way. I didn't move a muscle, nor did I breathe. Not until they started back up.

Chapter 15

Breathe in
Breathe out
Breathe in
Breathe out

Just one more, just one more, Jimmy. I opened my eyes to the ill-lit alleyway and a manipulative Carson standing before me. A shuffling sound to our right, near the end of the alley, interrupted my train of thought. Both our heads shot that way. I passed it off as a rodent and focused back on Carson.

"Like I said man," he began, "this is the last one."

His smug smirk made my blood boil.

"You said that last time."

"It will be," he said, raising his voice over mine.

I couldn't stop myself from lunging toward him, grabbing a handful of his shirt and shoving him against the dirty green dumpster sitting behind him. Holding his head in place, I prepared my right hand. Screw all of this; I'd kick his ass right here and now if it meant I would be free. He whipped out his phone and held the screen up for me to see. It was a video of me running out of the first store. An alarm blaring and a filled garbage bag in my hand. But it wasn't like that; I didn't have a choice. This was before he'd blackmailed me into robbing three more; this was the only one that had purpose. I had a reason, I truly did. I looked at the phone and then back at him. It took everything inside of me not to punch his teeth in that very moment. After that I could snatch his phone, crush it beneath my heel, and all of this could be over with. But knowing Carson, he probably already had the video backed up on a hard drive somewhere.

He smiled his conniving smile. He had me exactly where he wanted and worse, he knew it. My entire future, everything I'd worked for and cared about, sat in the palm of his hand, literally. He pulled out a small silver pistol with a black grip and shoved it in my stomach for me to grab. Grabbing that gun meant I was nothing more than a puppet under his strings. As dehumanizing as it was, I had no other choice. "I want that phone when I'm done." Backing up, I snatched the weapon from his hands and began to make my way through the alley. I paid no attention to the street rats scurrying past my feet. I hated this moment, the moment before it started. Before it was fear that flowed throughout my body, presenting any possible way this could go wrong.

Now, it's just guilt. Not just for what I was doing but for what I'd done. I looked up at the neon lights. So an antiques store this time? Reaching in my pocket I pulled out a mask. Just one more and all of this would be over. Just one more and I could go home. Slipping on my mask, I pushed through the doors. I scanned the store aisles quickly. No one else was inside. Normally I would've looked more thoroughly. Since this was the last job, I wanted it over as soon as possible. I promised Mom I'd cook dinner tonight. She deserved it after a long night of work.

Vintage items such as chairs and tables filled the floors. The walls, on the other hand, held various types of paintings and clocks for display. The man at the cash register smiled. That was until he saw my covered face. The mask told him what I was there to do. "Please don't do this," he said, "I need the money." The look on his face stuffed my stomach with a mix of guilt and regret. I wanted to leave right then and there but I couldn't. If I did, I too would lose everything. "I'm sorry," I said, pulling the empty pistol from my coat pocket and pointing it at him.

"Just give me everything and I'll be on my way," I said. The look on his made me feel horrible. "Just do it!" I said, pushing the pistol further in his direction. I tossed a garbage bag across the counter and watched him start to fill it up. Once it was full, he handed it to me and instantly held his hands back up. A huge gasp and the sound of glass breaking came from my right. There was a woman standing there. Her hand was perched across her daughter's chest in a defensive manner and her eyes were red and wide. "No, no, no please no," she mouthed. Her daughter had blond curls and blue eyes that hadn't blinked since she saw me.

There was a mirror behind them. I hadn't noticed it, but I had turned the gun in their direction. A little innocent girl and her mother. I dropped the gun and stared at myself in the mirror. Wondering how I'd got here. Just then I heard a shuffle from the register. I caught sight of the worker pulling something long from under his desk. It was a shotgun.

***

I watched him put on the mask and walk through the doors. Staring at the store in stunned disbelief, the neon lights illuminating the area, I didn't blink nor did I breathe. The other day, the article in the newspaper, and when Angela had asked us if we had heard of the recent robberies. I ducked my body back down, hiding behind the hood of the car on the other side of the road. It was Jimmy this entire time? No, no, not my Jimmy. Not the Jimmy who gave food to the homeless and who'd been volunteering at a church twice a month for the last five years. I was pulling hairs from my head like they were weeds as I sat in the grass, ignoring its moistness.

What could I do? Who could I call? What about Evalend, how would she reac- *Boom!* The sound, that horrible sound, erupted inside of the store. My body felt paralyzed. Not this, not like this. My body jolted up, tapping against the hood of the car I'd been hiding behind. Wide-eyed and open-mouthed I focused on the door. *Please Jimmy, please come out.* After a few seconds I slammed my fist against its hood, leaving a dent and setting off its alarm. *Jimmy.* The high-pitched sound rung in my ears. I covered my ears with my hand, but I wasn't moving until I saw my friend come through the doors. *JIMMY!* All of sudden, the doors opened up and Jimmy fell through them. It was as if the store had thrown him up. Managing to stay on his feet, he regained his posture and bolted down the road holding his shoulder. I started up a run of my own, being sure to keep my distance on the other side of the road. He had a black bag in his right hand which dropped a couple bills during his sprint. He ran like his life depended on it, taking huge steps and swinging the one arm he had available wildly.

He cut the corner taking a right down the road, and I checked both ways before following crossing the street. This was the block from earlier, where his car was parked. I followed him some more than ducked down again when I saw Carson waiting by Jimmy's car. He was pacing back and forth while patting his pants pockets with his hands. I creeped a bit closer and stood behind a tree. I was close enough to hear their conversation this time.

"What happened?! What was that noise?" I could tell it was Carson.

"What do you think it was?" Jimmy said, dropping the bag near Carson's feet and beginning to hold his right shoulder. "He took a shot at me while I was leaving; it only grazed me." He stopped applying pressure to his wound briefly, and pushed Carson against his own car door. "I Could've Died In There!" Jimmy said, pulling Carson forward and shoving him into the car door again. "Give me the phone!"

"Alright; jeez, man." I watched as Carson retrieved the phone from his bomber jacket pocket and held it out for him to grab. Jimmy instantly snatched it and stepped back, releasing Carson from his grip. They were in the middle of the street and it was dark out. I noticed a light within one of the houses behind the two flicker on. "What's the passcode?!" Jimmy shouted at Carson. "You didn't ask for that, you only said you wanted the phone," Carson laughed a bit; only he would think that was funny. Jimmy threw the phone to the ground and crushed it multiple times with his heel. Too caught up in their argument, they didn't realize that more and more lights in the surrounding houses were turning on. "HEY! WHAT THE HEL-"

That's when we all heard it - the police sirens. They were in the direction of the store - after hearing this, Carson took no time to run away while Jimmy desperately checked his pockets for his car keys. Finding them, he hopped in and started the engine before even closing the door. As he was about to pull off the porch lights behind me turned on, illuminating the entire area around me. An old man came through the door and yelled. He began to rant about how loud we were being but that didn't matter, he didn't matter. What mattered was that the lights were on, there were no cars near me, and I was exposed. And Jimmy was looking through the windshield directly at me. His eyes widened when he realized who I was.

Reading his lips, I could barely make out the word, "Jaxson." The sirens were getting closer and more people began to come outside from their homes. I flipped on my hood and took off as fast as I could, running down the block and taking a left. I heard Jimmy pull off in the opposite direction. I sprinted as fast as I could as the adrenaline still rushed through my veins. I cut through a park, hopped over a fence, and took off in the direction of my house. All the while the only thing that stayed on my mind was one question. Why, Jimmy? Why?

***

He'd got me. I was done for, but it wasn't because of the bullet. No, the bullet was only a graze. It was the blood. My blood, which was left all over the scene. My blood, which was probably on its way to be tested in a lab somewhere. Although I didn't know much about the process, I did know that on average the least amount of time I had was twenty-four hours. Twenty-four hours to figure something out. I slammed my fist upon my dashboard over and over again. It blinded me from how dangerous my acts were. I hated Carson with a passion, but most of all I hated myself. I released some more of my anger upon the pedal, slowly pushing it down more. My eyes were on the road, but I wasn't paying any attention.

The roads in front of me shifted into blurs the more I pushed down on the pedal. None of this would've happened if I hadn't done the first one. I slowed down just in time to make a hard right; I couldn't go to my house like this. Jaxson, I could go to-JAXSON. He saw me. I crashed my fist upon the dashboard again. Okay come on, think Jimmy. I could go to Angela's, but her dad was probably on high alert this time of night. I sighed as I released pressure from the gas tank. How did it all get this complicated? I looked to my left and for a few moments I was just staring at the trees passing me by. "And to think Mom," I looked in the mirror, back at what little I had left of myself, "I did it all for you."

Chapter 16

The tangerine hair, spotted cheek, sharp cheekbones, and those eyes I've seen a million times before: it was Jimmy. His face covered my TV screen. The words *WANTED* placed in bold under him. And no matter what the reporters said or whatever the little words passersby were saying, it was the only thing I noticed. I'd tried Jimmy's cell over a dozen times now and each went straight to voicemail. Pushing the bowl of cereal away from me, I got up and walked frantically in circles to ease my thoughts. Where could he be? Was he okay? Why wouldn't he pick up the damn phone. Grabbing my keys I made the spontaneous decision to search for him. With no hints of his whereabouts I left through the front door - the only thing in mind was the path to his house. Jimmy was smart, I was pretty sure he wouldn't go home. I wasn't counting on him to be there, but I wanted to see Evalend. Not just for a clue or any type of information that could lead me to him, but to check up on her in general.

I rang the doorbell and within five seconds max the door swung open - in all my years of coming here I'd never seen it open that fast. In addition, I'd never seen Evalend distraught as she did now. Her hair uncontrollable, eyes ruby red, and her eye bags indicated she hadn't had a drop of sleep all night. She grabbed both of my shoulders and began to talk in a panic, "Do you know where he is? What's going on? Is he hurt? What happened?" She unloaded a series of questions onto me. She spoke too fast for me to answer her questions. I couldn't blame her. I was looking into the face of a woman who didn't want to believe that she'd lost yet another man she loved.

I moved forward, opened my arms, and embraced her tightly. "I don't know. I don't know, I'm sorry. But I'm going to find him. I promise." Jimmy you idiot, what've you done? I backed up, and instructed her to calm down and await my return. I was going to find him, I didn't care how long it took me. I'd search every inch, alleyway, and corner of this damn town if I had to. I scrolled through my phone looking for Angela's name as my legs left Evalend's porch and met the sidewalk once again. Putting the phone to my ear, it rang and rang until it eventually went to voicemail. I tried again; still nothing. Come on, Jaxson. I knew him like the back of my hand, of all people I should know this. Where would I go? An idea popped in my head, the only one that made sense.

I moved through the woodland area covertly. Making sure not to hit any twigs hidden in the grass and dirt. *Scrape!* The noise came directly to me. I heard it again, *Scrape! Scrape!* It sounded like something being pulled roughly. I crouched down as I approached the clearing. Moving a low hanging branch out of my way granted me a view of a train car. An arm and leg could be seen poking out. The rest of the body was still engulfed inside the abandoned cart. The arm pulled something long, and whoever it belonged to cut a piece off and began to pull again. I recognized it as the same bandage that Coach made us use for injuries. *Snap!* Too busy focusing on what was going on in front of me, I forgot to watch the ground. Well, there went the element of surprise. Whoever it was stopped immediately and peeked out, revealing their face - it was Jimmy.

A sigh of relief escaped his mouth. "You had me going for a second there, Palmer," he laughed a bit. Only Jimmy could still find humor in a time like this. I had so many questions and no idea where to start. He turned around and started back on whatever he was doing. I moved forward to get a better look. He was wrapping a bandage around his wound. He bit it off the roll using his mouth, which we both knew wasn't the proper way to do so. I sat down on the other side of the train cart. My eyes were on the trees in front of me, but my attention never left Jimmy. I heard him pull the roll one more time before setting it down

"What happened, Jimmy?" I heard him shuffle around behind me.

"I thought I was doing the wrong things for a good reason," he replied.

"Care to explain a bit more?" I asked.

"I would, but I don't want you to remember me that way."

I turned around and stared at my best friend. Well, at least I thought it was him. The guy I was seeing looked completely different. His eyes were basically dead, and his infamous smirk was nowhere to be found. "What is that supposed to mean?" I asked. A few seconds later and no response. "Jimmy!" I shot out.

"I'm done for," he said. He dragged his palm down his face in frustration. I dropped down to the floor and back fell against the train.

"I can't go home, and Angela won't respond to any of my calls," he said. He continued on even though his words weren't making it to my ear. They were being trampled over by the thoughts in my mind. It wasn't supposed to be this way. The fact that I was about to lose another person bothered me to my core. I wanted anything but that.

"What if you ran?"

"And went where?"

"It's always been me and my mom, you know that." He still refused to face me. Not only did I know that, but I was also aware of how irrational it was. Jimmy is half of me, and there's no me without him. I knew that I'd never make it through another one of Ms. Shanley's boring lectures and I knew that I could never sit through another school field trip if he wasn't there. My fingers scraped against the rusted steel while my hand clenched into a fist. I couldn't lose him.

"I need a favor."

He finally looked at me, and his helpless eyes met mine.

"I need a couple sheets of paper and a pen."

"What for?"

"I want to write a letter to my mom and Angela."

"Anything else?"

"A sandwich with a couple of bottles of water. Oh, and since I'm going to jail and all, I hope you don't mind cutting off the edges."

I shook my head. It definitely was too soon to crack that joke, but he just couldn't help himself.

And off I went, making my way home. It was times like these where I felt the worst. A storm was coming, and there was absolutely nothing I could do about it. I could only stand there and take it. My pace sped up into a light jog. Jimmy reminded me a lot of my older brother; he was always there for me. This wasn't just another person, this was an actual piece of me. I began to run faster. He was damn near the only thing that had kept me from falling apart all of the years I'd been here. He was way more than a best friend; he was a brother to me.

Entering the house, I noticed Julia in my peripherals sitting on the couch. "Jaxson?" Ignoring her I darted up the stairs and into my room. She repeated it louder, but I didn't even acknowledge her, nor did I acknowledge her footsteps chasing me up the stairs. I turned to close the door on her and she stopped it with her hand. "What do you want!" I hollered from pure rage. I looked at the brown-skinned, curly-haired woman in front of me. She had on a phoenix necklace and she twiddled it with her fingers while smiling.

"Mom?"

I reached for her face slowly; it was really her and she was standing right there in front of me. "How're you-" the light flickered on in the hallway. When I blinked, she was replaced with a puzzled Julia. "Is everything okay out there?" Mark's voice echoed through the hall. I slammed the door and fell back to the floor. Was I going crazy? No, she was right there. I saw her take a breath. She even had on- The door reopened. Mark stood there with a face of concern. He walked up quickly and grabbed my shoulders. He strapped his arms across my back securely and set a hand in my hair. "I'm right here," he said.

"I'm right here."

Chapter 17

Dear Mom,

I know I haven't always been your trophy son. Truth is, I haven't been a decent one ever since Dad left. The day they kicked our door down and stripped us of him still haunts my mind. No matter how much I try to forget it, it's still there. I'm writing to you because we won't talk for a while. And just so you know, you didn't fail me, I failed you. Over the years you've sacrificed countless things for me. And in return, all I've done is give you heartache and pain that no mother should have to endure.

A teardrop slipped down my cheek and stained itself upon the sheet of paper.

Even though I never wanted to let you down like Dad did, it looks like the apple doesn't fall far from the tree after all. I don't want this haunting your mind while I'm away and because I know it will, I'm going to tell you why I did what I did. Three months ago, when you told me about the eviction notice I lied to you. I told you that I was fine and that I would just have to cope, but it was much more than that. I didn't want to leave behind Jaxson, Angela, the team, Coach, and everything I had, for that matter. So I went out and did what I thought was the "right" thing at the time. But now I realize it was the biggest mistake I've ever made, and there's nothing I can do about it. I love you, Mom. And I want to let you know that I appreciate every single boxing match you showed up to, the meals that you've made for me, and every time you kissed me goodnight. I don't know how long it will take but we will be together again.

-Love, Jimmy.

I took a nice long stare at the letter before sealing it in the pearl-white envelope and passing it, along with the one I'd written Angela, over to Jaxson. Letting go of those letters was one of the toughest things I'd ever done. After doing that, I knew that everything that was about to happen was true, and I was nowhere near ready for that. Standing up, I savored the sight of everything around me. It was an hour or so before dawn, and it had never been this peaceful in my life.

"If I had known that it was this beautiful at this time of day, I would've woken up earlier," I said.

"Hell, I probably would've even made it to school on time," I laughed a bit as I said this.

"No, you wouldn't have," he responded, cracking us both up.

I looked to my left, down the tracks, right where the sun would rise in about an hour or so. It was a shame I'd miss it. "You could always run," I heard Jaxson's voice behind me.

" Maybe so; I bet it would've been one hell of a ride," I said.

"Knowing you, it definitely would've," he responded.

I've never had a brother or sibling of any kind, but If I had, I wish they would've been something like him. Jaxson Palmer, my legendary partner in crime. I put my hand on his shoulder. "We've done a lot together. So do this one last thing with me."

At first it was easy, but the farther we traveled, the more difficult each step became. I felt the weight increase on my shoulders. Every time we inched closer I wanted to turn around and run for everything I was worth, but I couldn't. These were the ramifications of my choices. Therefore, I had to deal with it. It's astonishing how life can flip so fast. Just the other day I was with Angela, and we were debating over what movie to watch. We fought over the controller so much that she tipped over the popcorn and it spilled all over the floor. She laughed the entire time we cleaned up the mess. I'm still surprised she didn't break any glass by how deafening her cackle was. If I could go back, I'd relive that moment a thousand times over. I wished I could go back and do things differently. I wished she would pick up the phone.

I didn't notice the grassland beneath us turn into concrete as we made our way. We just kept moving forward. We didn't even acknowledge half of the cars or the people who passed us by. I thought about what would have happened if I'd never robbed the first store. Jaxson and I would probably be doing something completely different right about now, if it weren't for my mistakes. And even through it all, he still stood by me. We had no idea how this would end out, yet he still chose to walk into the fire with me, and I wouldn't have had it any other way. We weren't far now; only about a mile or two.

A lady pushing her baby in a carriage was about to pass us. She saw Jaxson and nodded at him with a smile, but when she saw me, she pulled back the carriage, bringing it to a halt. The worry scattered across her face stopped me in my tracks. I was never supposed to be this guy, not the one people were afraid of. I looked at Jaxson and wondered if he too looked at me differently. And if he did, then I was certain my mom and Angela did as well.

"Just a little bit longer," I said to him.

"You know, if it wasn't for you I wouldn't have survived around here," he started.

"You gave me something to look forward to every day, no matter how completely idiotic or kind of cool it was. Thank you," he said.

I held out my fist for him to bump it with his. "You ready for one more?" I asked.

"Always," he said while bumping his against mine.

City of Sycamore Police Department words stuck out on the side of the brick building.

"You know, I haven't been here since they took my dad away 10 years ago."

Jaxson looked at me, eyebrows furrowed and head tilting a bit.

"I owe it to you to tell you things like this. Since I never really talked about him," I finished.

"Well, if we're being honest, I'm adopted," he said.

"Dude, I've known that for years now."

"You look nothing like them," I laughed even harder.

"I should've seen that coming," he guffawed.

We both stared at the building for a while. It was open, exposing all of the workers who stayed overnight. I took a step forward and so did he; this continued until we made our way to the silver door. I held him back by stretching my right arm across his chest as he tried to walk through the doors with me. I grabbed the handle. He stepped forward to enter with me. My arm reached across his chest, stopping his step. I shook my head, disapproving of him moving forward anymore.

"You and Victoria make a really good couple."

"Maybe that's just another thing you've got to thank me for." Taking one last look at his face, I walked through the door. It wasn't as busy as it would be during the middle of the day, but there was a good amount of people crowding the area. However, weirdly no one shifted their heads to look at me, too busy looking at their papers or their phones. "Jeez, what's a guy have to do to get arrested around here," I mumbled. Scanning the room, I found a wooden board filled with wanted people. On that wall I found an extremely handsome face. I ripped it off and held it up for people to see. "Hey, does anyone think I could get a reprint?" I asked with comedic intent. Within a span of four seconds my head was banged against the wall and they handcuffed me from behind.

They dragged me off to a holding cell, where about five other guys were present; none looked over thirty and one had nodded off. I didn't know how they were able to sleep. The cell was chilly and smelled rancid. It was as if someone left dairy products around and didn't clean up for weeks. There was a brown liquid next to my shoe and dried blood stained on the walls behind me. As horrible as these features were, I used them to keep my thoughts at bay. I didn't want to think about all I've had in my life, and all I've lost.

Chapter 18

A one-week suspension was all I earned for cracking Carson straight in the jaw Monday morning. He didn't have to say any words to antagonize me, his face did that all by itself. The principal blabbered on about God knows what to me as I sat in this chair. Even though he was in the midst of reprimanding me, I could still sense some sympathy in his voice. Cutting him off by grabbing the suspension sheet, I crumpled it up in my backpack and left the office. An audience of high school students filled the area. I was receiving a bunch of unwanted attention I frankly didn't want. At least I'd got out of fourth period Calculous with Mr. Roberts.

The best thing about the class was Jimmy's snarky commentary over Mr. Roberts' methods of teaching. As many detentions as he'd given Jimmy, we could always tell he enjoyed the comments. Now that he'd gone, that class would never be the same. I exited through the doors, making my way to the side of the building, dropped my bags, and sat against the wall as my back slid down to the bottom. If it weren't for Victoria, I would've been on my way home. With no idea of how to handle any of this, I sat in the grass with only the growl of my stomach to accompany me. Although it was unplanned, I wish I had seen his conceited face after lunch.

In an hour and a half school would be over and I could be with Victoria. Merely the thought of her was enough to help still my thoughts. All I had to do was wait. Way easier said than done, considering not a moment passed where Jimmy wasn't on my mind. It was weird how the pain of loss worked. He was alive and well, yet it didn't feel like that. No matter if it was to a coffin or to a cell, it felt the same. Maybe calling Noah or even Mark for any chunk of advice would be beneficial. If only I didn't lack the motivation for an act that simple. In fact, I hardly even moved at all as I sat on top of the grass terrain. Just sitting there, watching cars and time pass me by.

Ringgg! The sound of the last bell traveled along the property. I pictured Victoria heading to my locker expecting me to be there; hopefully someone had passed the news along. I made sure to keep my distance from the school. Not too much to where I wouldn't be able to see Victoria as she came out, but enough so that I wouldn't be the first thing everyone else would see as they came out. Among the first twenty or so people to depart through the doors was Carson. He held what looked like an ice pack over his jaw and immediately got away from the school premises. My guess was he was trying to hide it from his buddies. He should be happy that there had been enough people around us to pull me away.

After minutes of waiting I recognized golden-brown, wavy hair emerging through the doors. She wasn't alone. She progressed through the doors with a crying Angela in her hands, the people around them granting them enough space to pass through. A sight which I'd never seen before. One of the many reasons Jimmy loved her so much was because of the constant tough and fearless attitude she brought with her everywhere she went. However, maybe the recent event was enough to break through her bulletproof walls. I caught their attention using my hand. With no chance to do this before, I deemed now a better time than ever. I dug into a small compartment on the front of my bookbag and pulled out the letter Jimmy wrote for her.

She held a tissue over her nose and never looked up; Victoria guided her the entire way. I was at a loss for words, I had no clue what to say so I instinctively leaned forward and embraced them both into my arms. It was something we all needed in this moment. Jimmy would want me to look after them both. "Who's going to cover the car rides now?" The light comment was a temporary relief for the grief. Even Angela could be heard laughing through her weeping. "He wanted me to give you something." I held out the letter for her. She reached out slowly and grabbed it carefully, shifting her eyes rapidly between me and the envelope. "He tried to call you a couple of times," I said.

She stumbled over her words and struggled to hold a straight face, "Yea I-I know. My dad took my phone away earl-" her sniffling and wiping her eyes broke up her statement a bit, "he took it away and made sure I stayed in the house when he saw Jimmy on the news," she finished. A car pulled up behind her and honked a couple of times; it was a blue Jeep that looked like an early 2000s model. The tinted windows fell down to reveal a middle-aged white man with a grave face and furrowed eyebrows. He stared each of us down. "Speak of the devil."

Angela peered down at the letter and looked back up. "You were an amazing friend to him," she took a couple of steps backward. "There wasn't a crazy adventure he told me about that didn't involve you in it." She turned around and walked towards the car.

I've never met Angela's mom, but I'm pretty sure Angela got her spirit from her. The only thing that she seemed to have inherited from her dad was blonde hair and blue eyes. And while hers were bright and filled with joy, his were just stale and cold. Victoria and I watched as the car pulled off and made a right, disappearing from our view.

"So how long did they give you for putting Carson in the nurse's office? You know most girlfriends would be pissed right about now. But luckily for you, I understand how much of a pain Carson Daniels is. If we're being honest, I wanted to crack him one myself while we were in PE. I just don't understand how someone can be so heartless," she said

"I was there that night; I saw both of them." Her gaze redirected itself on me.

"Carson was joking around as if we're some type of game or something," I clenched my fist. "The thought of it still pisses me off." I gritted my teeth. "Well, I'm happy you're safe and here with me," she said as she placed a hand on my chest. This simple act from anyone else wouldn't have changed anything. But since it was from her, it meant everything.

"I still have you," I said.

"And I'm not going anywhere," she responded.

***

Clang! Clang! The sharp noise arose from the back end of the house. Julia smiled and acknowledged the fact I'd just entered through the door. My guess was the school hadn't called Julia and informed her of my suspension yet. She pulled out a pre-made sandwich from the fridge and served it with a glass of water. "He's in the garage," she said. I thanked her for the meal and sat down at the countertop. After finishing the meal I dropped both the plate and the glass in the sink. On my way to the garage I heard Julia call me back. "Wait, Jaxson!" She stopped and held the marble countertop tightly. "Listen, the Mark in there is not the one you've known. The Mark in there is the one before-" She stopped herself. Closed her eyes and took a deep breath.

"It's the Mark I first met and fell in love with." Her white eyes turned scarlet. From the tone in her voice I could tell her words were genuine. "Well, I'm off to go meet him." I walked down the hallway escorted by enthusiasm, waiting to see what awaited me in the garage. The red Challenger's hood blocked Mark from my eyesight. When the door squeaked, announcing my arrival, whatever he tinkered with under the hood stopped. His fingers peeked over the hood and brought it down to a close. His shirt was covered with dirt and dust from the engine. Sweat stains could be seen under his armpits. And his head; it held no hair on top of it. I'd been so caught up in everything that I actually forgot about his condition. He cleaned his hands with a rag before throwing it over his shoulder, letting it dangle.

"I found out about my tumor too late," he said. "So I figured I'd at least slow it down. Maybe it'll give us enough time to finish this car up and get her running. Also, the school called about what happened today. I'm pretty sure you're about to have a lot of time on your hands," he chuckled. I was still more willing to believe that he was abducted by aliens than actually making a change this major. "Yeah, it was a rocky day, but that guy deserved it."

"Trust me, I know what that's like. Not all people though," he said, raising an eyebrow.

Was he trying to give me some advice?

"Maybe so."

"Dinner will be ready around seven; if you change fast enough we can probably put this new tire on," he said.

I nodded my head and began to head out.

"And Jaxson?"

I temporarily paused my movements.

"I'm sorry, about what happened to Jimmy. As much as he annoyed me, I liked the kid."

"I know you did, everyone did."

***

I stared at it. One of the things that haunted me the most in life. I figured I'd pass it on to Jaxson, I owed it to him. After all, it was the spark that had ignited the flame. I stared at the dent in the door. This was the best the mechanics could do to repair it. And compared to what it looked like before, it was a miracle. I glided my hand against the fractured steel, and with the cold feel came the excruciating memory.

"Mark, you better not drop us," she screamed with laughter as we pushed through the restaurant doors. I held her in my hands and twisted her around in a circle, admiring the brunette beauty wearing a pink skirt with a jean jacket covering it. I lifted her in the air a bit higher and kissed her stomach. It was only moments before when she had just told me she was pregnant; I'd never been happier. I placed her on the hood of my Mustang, grasped her waist, and pulled her closer. "I've loved you since I first laid eyes on you Junior year." I rested my forehead against hers. I truly was the luckiest guy in the world. "If only those were your wedding vows," she said, before playfully pushing me back a bit. She then after jumped off the hood, and blessed me with a heavenly kiss. One that stopped time and put me in a never-ending loop. Out of nowhere she broke off and opened the passenger door, teasing me with her eyes the entire time as she sat down. There wasn't a thing I wouldn't do for her and that baby. I made my way around to the driver's seat and strapped in. Resting my hands on the leather steering wheel, I noticed how bright the sun glared through the windshield.

Too caught up by Julia to notice anything, that's truly just how magical she was. I shifted the gear into drive and took off down the road. Her window was open, and I watched her hold her hand out and enjoy the rush provided by the wind. This perfect moment. I wouldn't mind spending my life like this. It looked like our dreams of driving all over the world letting the roads choose wherever we go would be stopped temporarily, but neither of us had any problem with it. "So what's our next stop?" I asked her while dialing down the volume knob. She flipped out her map that took up half of the dashboard; I could tell she had been waiting on that question all afternoon. "Well, I hear the food in Chicago's pretty good," she said while sliding her finger down the map. "Illinois it is." I added more pressure to the pedal. And there we went, driving dusk to dawn and dawn to dusk.

Chicago 2 Miles Ahead.

Seeing the sign my first thought was to wake up Julia. Even though the sky was pitch black, I knew she would wake up as ecstatic as always. That was another thing I loved about her - no matter where we were or what was going on, her eyes always lit up with curiosity. And this night was a very special one. Not only were the stars out, but the entire downtown area looked brilliant. It was littered with all types of different buildings, restaurants, and landmarks. Although it may have seemed like an everyday thing to everyone else, through the eyes of a small-town boy and girl it felt like we were finally in the movies we always pretended to be in when we were younger. The funny thing is that no matter what we passed along the way, my eyes never left her.

Maybe if I was paying more attention, I would've noticed the car speeding towards us out of her passenger window.

Wherever The Road Takes Us

Part 3

Chapter 19

Silence. The same cold emptiness that filled the air when Mom left and took my brothers and sister with her. And the same one that's stood between us every single night and day. His emotionless grey hair, horribly shaven beard, and hard stare that only seemed to care about the newspaper in front of him. I wouldn't even be exaggerating if I told you that I could disappear into thin air and he wouldn't even notice. No matter how much he walked, talked, or stared off into the distance, his gaze seemed to move right past me but never onto me.

He sat across from me, staring directly at his newspaper. I sat there for minutes. It may not have seemed like it, but this was my form of a distress signal. I wanted the slightest bit of acknowledgement from him. I wanted him to ask why I've been coming in so late or tell me he's been getting so many calls about me skipping school recently. But still there was nothing. Nothing at all to fill this void in my head. This silence; it was so loud. Even if I was outside of these walls, it was still the only thing I could still hear at times.

The only time I couldn't hear it was when I was with Jaxson. I don't know what it was about being around him. He simply made me feel valuable. He acknowledged me. But it wasn't because of my face or my figure; he actually listened to me. He cared about the words I had to say, and no matter how important or how futile they were, he treated each one the same. I felt so comfortable around him because I knew that he accepted me. I could be the most abnormal, weirdest version of myself anyone could possibly think of, and he'd only want to be closer to me. Which reminded me that I should get going right about now.

I opened the screen door. For a couple of seconds I stood at the doorway. I knew the odds were slim; in fact I knew it wasn't going to happen. I wanted to see if he would ask where I was going. Even though we both knew I was heading for school, some type of acknowledgement would have sufficed. Some type of sign that showed he cared, but still nothing. So I took a step out and let the screen door slam behind me. A load of relief fell from my shoulders as the stale air of our trailer was replaced with the freshness of the outside air. Taking a deep breath I inhaled it all, and exhaled slowly.

The sun began to peek over the horizon, and I stopped for a few seconds to admire it. I firmly believed in enjoying the small things in life, so the little sunrays of hope always helped start my day. There was more. More than this trailer park and this one-star town. I knew there was more. There was an entire world out there. One that was mine for the taking, and all I needed was a ride. Maybe my future adventures would give me something to write about. After absorbing as much sunlight as possible, I made my way over the dirt terrain, and off to Jaxson's house.

***

I laid down, my head in her lap, staring at the ceiling above me. She played with my hair; not in a playful manner, in a comforting way. She was there for me, no matter how little I spoke or even moved. As bad as I felt for putting her through this, I was very grateful overall. It'd been two days but nothing even felt slightly different. For some reason I was still waiting for some funny memes to appear in my messages from him, even though I knew it wasn't coming anytime soon. "You know," Vicky started, "Angela talked to Jimmy's mom and she got a mail saying his court date is next month," she said while sliding her hand from my hair to my cheek and gently caressing it. I directed my eyes to her concerned, lovely face.

She directed her gaze on me and lowered her head a bit. "Look babe, Jimmy's a first-time offender and all he did was rob a couple of stores. No one even got hurt. And maybe we could get Carson to confess. They were just some measly gas stations. He's going to be fine," she pleaded. Her words made sense; however she forgot one thing. Jimmy was eighteen years-old, no longer considered a minor. He'd be tried as an adult. She looked up from me and she instantly made the face she did when she was in deep thought. "Come on." She jumped out of the bed, dragging my arm with her. "Where are we going?" I asked.

"To change the way you feel."

"Ummm...the library?" We stood outside, staring at the neon sign that read *Open*. "Look, I'm not that much of a big reader," I said.

"Oh I know you aren't. Who is nowadays?" she said.

"But, I learned the best way to get away from your own life is to dip into someone else's for a while." She opened the door and held it for me to follow her through. I couldn't resist that smile. It was as if she knew how to catch my interest even when she wasn't trying. I caught the door right as it was about to close.

Based off the outside of the place, I thought it would be ancient or abandoned. Surprisingly enough, the interior actually caught me off guard. The bookshelves and tables were all wooden and spotless, the lights did a great job luminating the area, and even though it wasn't even noon yet there was already a pretty decent crowd. "Do you come here often?" I asked Victoria. "All the time," answered a new, senile voice coming from our right. There was a lady, possibly in her 60s, standing behind a cash register that was filled with all sorts of accessories such as bookmarks, pencil sharpeners, mints, etc. "Maybe a little too much," she commented. "But you know what they say," she continued, and then both Victoria and the lady said, "Too much reading is never enough," as if they'd practiced this before.

"Good morning, Mrs. Taylor," Victoria cheered. Her cute smile dragged me into a daydream. "Good morning there Vicky; and, who's your friend you brought along?" she asked, shifting her focus from Victoria to me. Before I could even get a word out, she grabbed my arm and pulled me right next to her hastily. "This is Jaxson," she said. I pulled up one of my hands to wave and said, "Hi, it's nice to meet you." She looked at me and when she heard my name a bolt of realization crossed her face. "Ohh. You're *theee* Jaxson? I've heard so much about you," she said. "Oh, so you have now?" I turned my face to find a seemingly embarrassed Victoria, with burning cheeks, who was now shifting her weight from side to side. "What have you heard?" I asked. "Nothing!" shouted Victoria as she guided me towards the books. "We'll be back soon!" she said back to Mrs. Taylor. "No, please! Take your time," the lady gave in response.

Books hadn't always been my thing but for Victoria it was a completely different story. I'd heard her talk about how she liked to read and write. I just never knew it brought out this much excitement from within her. She couldn't keep her hands to herself as she rushed from one book to another. She basically burned through the aisles, constantly picking up one book, reading its description, and then moving to the next one. Meanwhile, I was still trying to find what genre I liked. I skipped past most until I saw a black label with red words that said "Thriller/Mystery." This was the one that caught my attention the most.

This section was about medium-sized and had a polyester rug in front of it. There were a lot of captivating names such as, "Lies Dressed in White," and, "Wonder In Apartment B." They all sounded good but then, out of the corner of my eye, I noticed one that stuck out like a sore thumb. It had a candlelight orange color and for some reason just seemed interesting to me. I picked it up and immediately noticed how smooth the cover was. Its title was "Dying Breed," and it turned out this book actually wasn't supposed to be sitting there. It was a Poetry book sitting in the Thriller section.

On my way to return it to its proper place, an idea came across my mind. Poetry has always been a thing I never minded reading. Most of it was usually short, simple, and sweet. Checking the price, it read $15.00. Technically speaking, it was still a book. I searched around for Victoria to inform her of my accomplishment. She wasn't near any of the books, nor was she by the tables. I kept scouring around, moving to the back-right corner of the building where there was actually a computer section I had no knowledge of.

These weren't the traditional bulky, white, prehistoric computers that one usually expects from a typical library. These were Chromebooks, locked down to the black table beneath them. It was easy to spot her. Her back was towards me, and her head rested on her fist. She was staring directly into the screen and didn't move an inch. I crept up on her, and the closer I got, the more I recognized the site she was on. She was on Google Docs, looking at multiple different documents. "And what're these?" I whispered into her ear. She tried to exit out of the tab immediately while repeating it was nothing. I prevented her from doing so by stopping her hand with mine.

"By that reaction it doesn't seem like nothing."

"They're just some poems and stories I wrote," she mumbled, "it's nothing really."

"You write?"

"I told you this before," she babbled.

"You said you used to write when you were younger. Not that you still do."

I released her hand and quietly sat down next to her.

"Well, now you have to let me take a look at some," I said, trying to convince her.

"Nooooooo," she groaned. Shortly after this, she noticed the book sitting in my hands.

"It looks like you got what you needed. We can get going now," she said, beginning to close the Chromebook. I stopped it by placing my hand on the pad before it collapsed.

"Come on, Just a peek?" I bargained

"Fine," she gave in. "But you have until I come back from the bathroom." She got up and promptly made her way to the women's room. I scrolled through the different documents, trying to make a solid decision. I was getting desperate so I just clicked on the shortest one I could find. The writing was complex and interesting. Although it was difficult to interpret, I could tell it was about loss. More specifically, about a musician who I guess had gone deaf. And he feels that now since he lost his music he's lost everything. I was nearing the end.

So close my casket and take me home,
I've lost my music, for I've lost my-

The closing of the laptop in my face interrupted me from the ending and teased my interest. Her hand was placed firmly on top, and my eyes followed it up to her face. I didn't think it was possible. Yet, I'd found another thing I loved about her.

Chapter 20

The old, rusted metal made a loud cranking noise as Mark began to jack up the vehicle. It was about 10:00 in the morning and we were in the middle of replacing the front right tire of my soon-to-be car. As more and more days passed by, I only seemed to have more time to burn - and most of it was spent thinking about Jimmy. Just the questions of what he was doing consumed my mind 24/7. Besides that I was just grateful that he didn't get hurt or worse. A couple of coughs escaped Mark's throat. However, these weren't regular ones. I'd been noticing them get a little raspier each day that passed by.

He faced a hand in my direction, stopping my advancement towards him. He dropped his hand, and his breathing became regular. "I'm good," he claimed. I didn't believe this for a second. Each day his skin grew lighter and his body weight was depleting. None of these changes were too noticeable, however.

"Hey, what do you say we take a break and get some food?" I asked him.

He looked a bit surprised, "Sure, Julia will be home so-"

"It's fine," I said, cutting him off. "It can just be us two."

I'm quite sure this moment was extremely awkward for both of us. Considering the fact that we'd never gone out alone together before. And the few times we did go out, Julia was always with us. But here, in this burger shack, it was only the two of us. We'd both ordered cheeseburgers with fries, and now we were just waiting. It wasn't long before he sat forward from his yellow booth seat and placed his jumpy hands on the peeled, brown table.

"You know. I'm envious of you and Jimmy," he said.

"What do you mean?" I asked, blinking my eyebrows in confusion.

"I had a friend like that once. We would always raise hell together. You can even ask Julia; I bet she still remembers him," he said, while looking off to the side and laughing a bit afterwards.

"What was his name?" I asked.

"Dennis. Dennisssss," he sounded as if he was thinking.

"Johnson. Dennis Johnson," he remembered.

"And where's he now?"

"Last time I checked he works in sales in Manhattan, I believe," he answered.

"Well anyway, the reason I brought it up is because I know what it can be like to lose someone," he began to look at the table.

"Now, the way I've dealt with it hasn't always been ideal, and that's why I'm talking to you now. I don't want you to make the same mistakes I did," he said.

The more and more we talked, the more I sensed sincerity in his eyes. Maybe it was possible that he did care about what he was saying. "I've done a lot of things wrong. But if I'm going to die, I at least want to do that right," he said, while reaching into his pocket and pulling out a key. "The car's not the only thing that'll be yours when I'm gone."

***

My eyes were glued to the computer screen in front of me. One spark. One start. One story. That was all I needed. I came up with millions every week. Now that it was time to release one from the chains of my mind, there was nothing. Every word that was emitted by my fingers was soon deleted by insecurities. It was as if nothing I wrote had a place. I began to wonder why I was even doing this. Jaxson said I had the "gift of words" and that wasted talent was a horrible thing. I'm 90% sure he'd got that off of an old movie. Nevertheless, I didn't come here for no reason.

Come on, Victoria. All I had to do was just bring one to life. Even if it was bad, as long as it was something. After opening up a new document I began to type out my first sentence, "**It may be hard for most people to understand this, but there's a power in letting go.**"

***

Knowing you just threw your entire life away is one thing. Knowing you just threw your entire life away with no distractions at all except a grey wall, which separated me from the next inmate, was exceedingly worse. All of the hours my mom had put in for me to go to school and the scholarship I had earned - all gone. And to add insult to injury, there was no way I could get them back. There was no way I could see Jaxson or Angela. It was just me, my cell, and this small red copy of Webster's dictionary.

This was one of the few distractions I possessed, and it wasn't bad. Turns out there are words for things I've never thought of. For example, Sonder. Sonder meant the realization that every random person you encounter, no matter where you are, has a life as intricate and crazy as yours.

At first, I thought this was something pretty obvious and stupid to make a word out of. Now I realize just how factual and eye-opening it was; that's probably only because of the situation I'm in. For some reason they gave me a trial, which I believe is pointless because it's pretty evident how guilty I am after all. The bed my back lay on was stiff and cold. No matter how many times I slept on it, it just never seemed to warm up. Maybe that was because I kept expecting it to be my bed from home. The one my mom and I would watch comedies on, the one Jaxson managed to always drop Cheetos on, and the one Angela never wanted to leave. I knew I'd upset a ton of people with this stunt, yet my mind only wondered what those three thought of me at this moment.

Ding! Ding! Ding! This noise coming from my left caught my attention. It was a guard standing on the other side of the steel bars, "Delgado. You've got a visitor." Excitement shot me up from the ground.

"Who is it?"

"I assume it's your mother."

Mom. On one hand I was ecstatic, on the other I was nervous. I'd never in my life imagined that she would have to see me like this. Well, they say there's a first time for everything after all. I planted my foot next to the cell entrance and waited for him to open it. When it did open, he slapped cuffs onto my wrists and grasped my back before we left. The cells were filled with men of all different colors, shapes and sizes. I didn't know anything about them, besides the fact that they too had screwed up as bad as me. Half of them were staring at me while the others were either working out or trying to sleep, all wearing the same bright orange jumpsuit.

Lines of empty booths filled the room. Some had other inmates talking through a phone to whatever loved one was on the other side, while others were desolate. There was one with a woman on the other side. Her makeup smeared down her cheeks. Once he unlocked my cuffs, I walked towards the booth seat. Was she disappointed in me? Did she hate me? All those years of her working double shifts out of the window. All because I'd messed up. Eventually I found enough strength to sit down and put the phone to my ear.

I remember when I was younger and my mom brought me to see my father. And now she had to look at me the same way we looked at him ten years ago. The sniffles I heard through the phone let me know how difficult this must have been for her. My eyes couldn't bear to look up. "Jimmy," was her first word,; because of her broken voice you could barely make it out. Hearing her like this felt like someone was holding a torch to my heart. "Mom," I answered, still not looking up. "You know, you didn't have to do that for me. I was fine, you could've just -" she stopped herself. She gripped the phone tightly in her hand and dug her flat palm into her forehead. I heard her take deep breaths over the phone and regain her posture.

"How're they treating you in here?"

"Well. The food's nothing like yours, that's for sure." Comedy has always been a self-defense of mine. Only now it didn't seem to have much effect.

"They wouldn't allow me to bring any. They're afraid of people trying to smuggle things in."

I exhaled slowly. My eyes stuck to the cold steel table like glue.

"I picked out a suit for you. It's your just your size and it even has-"

"Stop. Just stop, Mom." I took the phone off my ear and held it against my forehead for a second to recollect my thoughts. After a few seconds I returned it.

"We both know where I'm going."

She began to shake her head back and forward slightly.

"No…no there could be some kind of mistake-"

"Mom," I said, trying to get her to stop.

"You were the only one who even got hurt-"

"Mom."

"You're just a kid for God's sake, they can't take-"

"Mom!"

This time she stopped. I looked through the clear glass and at her pale, grief-filled face.

"I did it, Mom. I did it," I placed a hand on the glass.

"Delgado!" I heard the voice and footsteps approach me. Still, I ignored them.

She placed hers back and said, "I love you."

No matter how loud they hollered or how hard they grabbed me, my mother was the only thing that mattered. I admired her black hair, freckled face, and crystal eyes because I wouldn't be seeing them around too often. "I love you too, Mom," I mouthed, and even as they pulled me away, my sight never left her distraught face.

Chapter 21

Nothing could take my attention away from him as he lay there while his breathing struggled to stay consistent. My sweet, sweet Mark. The years hadn't been anything like what we dreamt of when we were teens. Still, we'd had each other through them all. While caressing his chin, I reminisced on the days when there was nobody besides me, him, and the open road. Even though that dream shriveled up, our love was far from old. And it's been that way since my parents kicked me out. I planted my head upon his once bulky, now frail chest. Every day his body grew feebler. The worst part about this was that I noticed every change, no matter how small the detail or curvature.

It was a burden on my heart to see him this way. To think that our time would be ending soon impacted daily life in every way. There wasn't much I wanted to do anymore. I had my suspicions that he knew about his illness long before we entered that doctor's office. In fact, I was almost certain he did. If he did decide that now was his time to go, as much as I hated it, I couldn't blame him. It isn't hard to see that he still blamed himself all of the time. Not only for what he'd done but for how he handled it as well. I sat up in our bed and lay my back against the wooden bedpost. What am I going to do when your time is up?

What about our dream of traveling the world? What of trying to have another baby? I knew how selfish and unreasonable it was to ask him all this, but I couldn't digest that these things will never happen.

***

"If what you're about to tell me is really that bad I hope you're covering the bill." The waitress had just dropped off a cup of hot chocolate for both of us. Victoria folded her hands around her cup as she smiled, displaying her wall of white teeth. We were sitting inside of a breakfast diner, one that wasn't Joe's for once. This action made me feel like I'd betrayed him.

"Of course." Today's the day I tell her.

"Victoria…"

A sharp exhale was released from my mouth before I bluntly said, "I'm adopted…and Mark has cancer." Like a bandage from a wound, my burden was now released. I was a strong believer in freeing my skeletons swiftly. A mouthful of hot chocolate shot out of her mouth and back in the mug. Luckily for her, none of it spilled on her white shirt which was covered by a denim jacket. After a few coughs her face turned upwards to me.

"Is this a joke or are you serious?"

I shook my head slightly back and forward.

"I'm being honest."

She dropped her mug on the table.

"I'm sorry. I didn't know how to tell you. It all happened so fast."

"So the one you told me about. That hurt you and didn't want you to draw. Was that your real father or the one that's-"

"The one I live with now."

She stretched her hands out on the table. It was a bit of an abnormal act, but I understood that everyone had their own way of processing information. She did after all just get trainloads thrown at her. Moments later, she exhaled and relaxed her elbows.

"How does this make you feel?"

"At first it wasn't that bad, considering all he's done. Now that I've gotten to know him more as a person... I don't want this to happen." I sat up more in my seat and let my arms fall on the table. With her here, I felt the ability to be vulnerable. To release the whispers that roamed my mind all night long. "Mark and Julia have been the only real parent figures in my life since my actual parents-"

My fists clenched and my eyes closed momentarily. Thinking about it was something I'd gotten accustomed to. However, saying it was a harder act to pull off. My eyes reopened.

"Passed. Ever since they passed. For years I've watched him drink himself silly till he couldn't walk anymore. For years he's hated the sight of me and now he's someone else. I just don't understand it." They weren't words of hatred or anger. They were desperate and full of confusion. I had so many unanswered questions. One which slipped out of my mouth even though it was meant for my thoughts, "You know what I don't get? Why, after everything he's done, she's still with him. Julia stayed by his side no matter how much he wronged us. She's still there!" This time I blurted all these out. It wasn't enough to capture the attention of the entire restaurant. It was enough to make the people surrounding us quiet down. Frustration began to build up inside of me. I dug my head into my hand.

After a few moments of silence, she got up, walked over to my side of the booth, and sat down right beside me. She firmly stopped my foot which had been clicking against the ground repeatedly; I hadn't even noticed. Then, she lifted my head from my hand and replaced it with hers instead. She rested her head on my shoulder. The audience around us slowly began to resume their original conversations. And there I was again, looking out of another window on another gloomy day. It wasn't alone this time. She was with me.

"And I do have a brother. His name's Noah. Luckily for him, he's miles and miles away. I think about him every day. He's the only piece I have left of the life I used to love. And I barely have him anymore."

"My father was the one who gave me those bruises."

My attention shifted over to her. I'd always inferred it was him who did it, I just didn't want to believe it. "You may be wondering what kind of father would do that to his daughter. I ask myself that every day." Her hands stroked my arms slowly.

"I guess family issues are another thing we have in common."

We somehow found humor in this. After our laughter faded, she opened up again.

"Would you like to know what thought gives me comfort?"

"Do I even have a choice?" I questioned.

She playfully slapped her hand against my chest and laughed,

"Knowing that one day we'll be a million miles away."

***

"All right." The hood fell against the body of the car as he began to make his way around to the passenger side of the car. He dropped down on the leather seat and said, "Start her up," pointing at the keyhole. My hands gripped the steering wheel. I entered the key into the hole and twisted it to the right. After a few seconds of the car struggling to start, the roar of the engine filled the void. "Wooo!" shouted Mark, grasping my shoulders out of excitement. I had never seen him this happy before. "It's all yours." Still having a hard time believing this, my hand slapped against the dashboard and wiped away the little dust that stood left. I'd been wanting a car since I got my license two years ago. "Now you've got something to pick up that pretty girl with," he raised an eyebrow at me and shook a finger towards me. Little did he know that pulling up in this beauty and impressing her was the first thing I'd thought about as soon as the engine started up.

He shoved his arms to his mouth and began to cough and wheeze horribly into them. Usually these ended after a few seconds; however, this time was different. It lasted longer and sounded horrible. I couldn't help but begin to worry. "Are you okay?" He placed his hand against the passenger window for support as he let out one final cough into his arm. "I'm good," he responded, opening the car door and letting himself out. I watched him struggle to climb out of the car. It was evident that his condition was only getting worse, yet he seemed to only smile more for some reason. None of it made sense. "Oh come on, don't worry about me. You need to be worried about the paint job."

"Seriously?"

"Yeah, red was my color. Now, this is *your* car." He made his way to the door. "Take a shower and get dressed up. We'll leave to get the supplies after breakfast," he said as he left the garage. I heard him pat the door as he returned momentarily. "Oh, and don't worry about the price either, I know a guy who owes me a favor or two."

Chapter 22

"Are we there yet?"

"No. Just a few more feet," Jaxson mumbled into my ear. We weren't far from his front door when he cupped his hands around my eyes, so I knew whatever this "surprise" was had to be near his house. "3, 2, 1, Voila!" he exclaimed, releasing his hold on my face. It was his garage. The door opened and inside there was a blazing red Challenger. Next to it there were a couple of paint cans that hadn't been opened.

"Is this...no way." I turned around to look at him while slightly backing up towards the garage.

"There's no way this is yours."

He smiled and nodded his head up and down. I whirled back around to get a better view while stopping before the entry. I heard him step up, and felt him wrap his arms around my waist. He rested his chin on my shoulder.

"So, I'm guessing this paint is the reason you were so specific about my clothing."

He took my hand and we walked closer to the car. "That, and to see you out of a sweater for once. Although a long-sleeve shirt is still a bit disappointing." He stretched out my arm sleeve a bit and then let it flap back against my skin.

"What can I say? I like to learn."

I slowly slid my hand against the hood, "How did you even pay for this?"

"I didn't. It was Mark's."

"He paid for this," I questioned gazing over my shoulder at him.

"No. It was somewhat of a hand-me-down. Nevertheless, it's mine now." He paced around the back of the car, "And I can already see you in my passenger seat."

Little did he know in a small corner of my mind I was already thinking about our first road trip. Preferably to one of the places I had in my scrapbook. I've been cutting out different national parks out of catalogs and gluing them in my scrapbook for years now. It was my own type of bucket list. Yosemite National Park all the way out in California was at the top. I picked up one of the paint cans and swung it around to see.

"You do know that our finished product is going to look vastly different than one done by actual professionals, right?"

He picked up two paintbrushes, "Luckily for us, I'm not looking for anything too special," he responded.

"So, let's get started."

For three hours I had more fun with him than I'd had in the whole week. We were too busy goofing around, and occasionally taking short make-out breaks, to even make a good amount of progress. I was almost finished with the front passenger door when he decided it would be funny to flick his paintbrush at me, leaving a trail of black spots on my shirt. To justify the actions he held his hands in the air, while slowly backing up, and said, "Hey, to be fair I did tell you to wear clothes you don't care about after all."

It was backed up by a smile, and as mad as I wanted to be, I couldn't ignore how cute it was. I lunged toward him and slashed my paintbrush diagonally across his yellow T-shirt. When he looked down, I covered my mouth and laughed into my hand. A big smile appeared across his face, "It's on." I was barely out of the garage when he swiftly took a hold of my waist and lifted me in the air. Letting my head back, I roared in laughter whilst kicking in a playful attempt to escape his grasp. If I was being honest, there was something about being in his control that gave me a slight guilty pleasure.

That was until I noticed he was carrying me towards an open paint can. I had no idea what he was planning but I didn't want to find out. "Jaxson! Wait!" As nervous, and slightly frightened, as I was, I couldn't help but laugh the closer we got. "Well, you two are definitely getting a lot done." Mrs. Palmer leaned against the doorway with a rag in her hand. Her eyebrows rose sarcastically as she grinned in anticipation of our answer. Jaxson carefully set me down and began to pat his hands against his sides.

"Would you believe me if I told you we were making some progress?"

"Hmmmm, perhaps some small, small amount is believable. Do you two have anything in mind for dinner?"

"Actually is alfredo fine?" Jaxson questioned. I expected an answer out of him because his stomach growls had basically been echoing off the garage walls.

"Linguine or penne?"

"Just alfredo is fine," he clarified.

A short glance in her eyes revealed she was struggling containing her laughter just as much as I was. Her head dropped to the floor and chuckles broke free through her teeth. Seeing her let it out made it easier for me to join her.

"What's so funny?"

I could hear the confusion in his voice.

I grabbed onto his forearm. "She's asking what type of alfredo, silly."

"Umm…Italian."

Mrs. Palmer broke out even more. Through my own amusement I was barely able to utter the words, "Linguine is just fine."

As she left the scene, Jaxson still struggled to figure out what we'd found humor in it. Mid-speech I cupped my hand around the back of his neck and pulled him in closer to me. Our foreheads met and I felt his warmth in the air. "It's nothing babe." My hand slowly slid up to his right cheek. "Nothing at all." And just as I was about to place my lips on his, he beat me to the act. Nothing more than him mattered in this everlasting moment. This was the only moment where I could not be moving an inch, yet feel so empowered. His taste was enchanting, and this friction between us was unbelievably satisfying. I slightly hated him for breaking away as he curled my hair behind my ear. He opened his mouth, "And they said the perfect girl doesn't exist."

Chapter 23

Before leaving through my room door, I took one last look at myself in the mirror. Observing the dark grey, fitted suit I had on which was complemented by a black tie. I was surprised Mark even had a suit, let alone one that fitted me. Today, like many others, would be a tough one. Acknowledging this, I grabbed the keys to my new car, which I still wasn't used to having, and made my way downstairs for some food. "We can just take you there if you want," Mark smiled, hiding his true concern underneath it. "And just neglect the days of work we put into this bad boy?" I said, pointing my thumb behind me at the open garage, with the finished product of our paint job within it. "No way."

    I twisted around and headed towards my new car. "Besides, I have a couple of people to pick up anyway," I insisted. Stopping at the car I analyzed it. For people who had never painted a car before, it wasn't bad at all. There were some imperfections caused by Mark and I; meanwhile Victoria did an exceptionally good job on the vinyl stripes. They started on the trunk and traveled across the hood and down to the Challenger emblem. Originally, I thought it was unnecessary of her to cut out the stripes in cardboard and then do her best to align them against the car and color them in. But, now that I saw the final project, I didn't mind it at all.

    I gripped the leather steering wheel firmly, caressing the sides and slipping my hands down to the keyhole. If only Jim could see me now. Knowing him, he'd probably try to initiate some form of street race. I opened my phone, slid down to Victoria's name, and called her. After a few rings she answered with a, "Hello." Normally it was a "Heyyy babe," or something like that but today didn't exactly set the mood for that.

"Hey, Are you and Angela ready?"

"Yeah, she's with me. She's not holding up too well. Do you think you could drop her off shortly after? Her dad doesn't know that she's going today."

"Yeah, yeah that's fine. I'll be over in a few."

***

"All rise!" the female bailiff's voice echoed across the courtroom. Mark, Julia, Victoria, Jimmy, Ms. Delgado, and I all stood along with everyone else in the courtroom. A black man, with grey hair scattered across his hair and beard, came out wearing a standard judicial robe and stood behind his stand. "The Court of the Second Judicial Circuit, Criminal Division, is now in session, the Honorable Judge Davis presiding," announced the bailiff.

"Everyone but the jury may be seated," said the judge. When he stated this, everyone sat down. He then faced the woman. "Mrs. Park, please swear in this jury."

"Please raise your right hand," she requested of the judge.

I could feel my heart thump against my chest. If this was how nervous I felt, I could only imagine how Jimmy and his mom were. This was the first time I'd ever seen Jimmy like this. Evalend and Angela sat away from us near the front. My guess was they'd just wanted to be as close to him as possible. Judge Davis stayed standing and raised his right hand. "Do you solemnly swear or affirm that you will truly listen to this case and render a true verdict and a fair sentence as to this defendant?"

"I do."

"Your Honor, today's case is The State of Illinois versus Jimmy Delgado."

"Is the prosecution ready?"

Jimmy getting into trouble was always inevitable, but never did I guess it would be like this. My glance shifted left and focused on Angela and Ms. Delgado. No matter what the crowd was instructed to do, they never looked away from Jimmy. He was a couple rows ahead of them, the back of his grey suit facing the crowd. It was tight on him. It looked like it would tear across his back any second. The trial moved on; sadly to say there wasn't much that could be done. Everyone knew that Jimmy had done it. If anything, we were praying his punishment wouldn't be too cruel Technically speaking Jimmy was eighteen, which means he wouldn't be receiving the same punishment as a minor. "Yes, Your Honor," responded one of the prosecuting attorneys seated on the right of the room, about five rows ahead of us. The prosecutor was a tall man. He was white and carried an unfriendly, stern look under his glasses. He then adjusted one of his buttons on his noticeably tight suit, and they took their seats. "Is the defense ready?" The judge looked at Jimmy and his attorney.

"Yes, Your Honor," replied Jimmy's attorney. He was a short man with a stubby figure. The lights reflected off of his bald, sweaty head which he frantically patted with a towelette. Could anybody really blame him? This wasn't a "prove your innocence" trial. The evidence was real and incredibly incriminating. None of us here held a slither of hope that he would be found innocent. We all watched as they sank into their seats, and after a few moments we did as well.

The entire prosecution process was pitiful. The air was filled with little-to-no hope for Jimmy Delgado. The prosecutors were loud, and made Jimmy out to seem like a delinquent any chance they had. And as for his defense, there was practically none. His state-given attorney stumbled over his words, which was hard to believe since he was a lawyer. Looking around, I needed somewhat of a distraction.

Angela and Ms. Delgado had interlocked their hands and did their best to hide their tears. Jimmy himself kept his gaze at the floor the entire time. He wasn't saying much, nor did his body expression even change a tad. I couldn't help but to wonder a bit as to what he was going through mentally. Mark, who was looking a little paler than usual, and Julia, were locked into the trial. His eyes struggled to stay open. I patted on his shoulder and mouthed the words, "You okay?" a couple of times. Each time he responded by nodding his head and focusing on the trial. Meanwhile, Victoria seemed to be more focused on me than anything. She even reached her hand over to stop my unintentionally moving leg that was clicking against the floor and causing a minor disruption. Realizing this, I looked up to see if it had drawn too much attention. And sure enough, about seven or so faces were staring at me. Shortly after my leg stopped they all turned back around and the trial resumed. Her nimble hand held on to me ,and our fingers wrapped around each other.

"Everything's going to be okay," she reassured me. After that, she kissed me on my left cheek and kept her head on my shoulder. I didn't know whether to believe this or not. All I did know was that I just wanted to talk to him. If he wasn't going to be there at our senior-year graduation, and if I wouldn't get another ride in his red GMC truck which held so many memories, then one talk would suffice. It didn't matter if it was two minutes or even two seconds.

***

She worked fifty hours a week. Every week for four years. All for me to attend school with the people I loved, and be able to take Angela out on the best dates possible. And this was it. This was how I repaid her. Sitting in a courtroom, too ashamed to turn around and face any of my loved ones. Too guilty to even make an attempt against everything they said about me. Mainly because a part of me believed them. Maybe I deserved whatever was coming my way. Nonetheless, I'd kill to have one late-night dinner with Mom or movie with Angela. It could even be The Notebook - I wouldn't mind. Anything to feel her heat and hear her voice again. All that accompanied me now were my own self-destructive thoughts.

The sound of someone weeping soared through the air. It came directly from behind me. I knew it was somewhat disrespectful to take your attention away from the trial, especially if it was yours, but I just had to find out who it belonged to. I grabbed the back of my chair and twisted around quickly. The chair bottom screeched against the wooden floor. A few rows back sat Mom and Angela. They sat there with trembling chins, rapidly streaming tears, and trying to force a smile back at me. Mom's makeup had worn off due to the amount of tears that escaped her eyes. She was wearing a familiar black dress; I couldn't put my finger on it, but I was sure I'd seen it before.

And Angela looked as beautiful as always. She had on black pants and a white dress shirt. Through her trembling lips I could make out the words, "I love you." The two women reminded me of the perfect life I'd had not too long ago. They always took care of me and did their best to make sure I stayed out of trouble. Every single boxing match I'd had I could count on them to be there, and even if one couldn't make it, I would basically spend the night recalling every detail.   My attorney, Mr. Jones, nudged me on the shoulder. Apparently, they'd been calling my name and I was too distracted to notice. After taking one last glance at them I turned around. Fixing this all was the only thing I wanted. "Defense, you may call your next witness to the stand." The judge stared both my attorney and me down. My attorney then stood up out of his seat, leaving his index finger touching the wooden table below him. "Thank you, Your Honor. I now call to the stand Jimmy Delgado."

An immense silence befell the courtroom. The sound of my heels clicking against the floor filled the courtroom. Resting at the stand, I was met with around thirty faces, but for some reason it felt like hundreds. Even so, only a few mattered. The one of my trembling mother, wonderful lover, and my true best friend. Knowing that my world was about to change, I closed my eyes and took a deep breath. Blessed to even be in the same room as the people I held dearest. Placing my hands on the stand I felt its solid wood exterior. Looking up, I cherished the faces of everyone, even Jaxson's parents who I'd barely ever talked to. Now confident in my answer I tilted over towards the mic.

"Your Honor, I plead guilty."

Chapter 24

Walking out of that courtroom would've been a lot easier if Jimmy had been beside us. Either way, for some strange reason I thought he'd be fine. I'd never seen someone smile while they plead guilty before. Yet, it wasn't a smile of laughter. It was sudden, small, and genuine. Walking out, I still held Victoria's nimble hand in mine. This was about the only thing that had kept me sane throughout this trial. Ten years in prison with parole after five. Sycamore's boxing star would probably be all over the news tomorrow. And people would make assumptions about him, but their opinions didn't matter. Only the people who knew Jimmy knew the truth behind his actions. He wasn't some criminal that robbed stores for the fun of it. He was just a scared teenager who made a stupid decision; nothing more nothing less.

"I appreciate you two coming out today," I thanked Mark and Julia, who were holding each other while heading to their car. They both turned around. "It was not a problem at all, honestly," Julia comforted me. I looked over at Mark, who was clutching his eyes shut, and a trickle of sweat slipped down from his hairless head and over his eye. The more I studied the way they held each other, I realized it wasn't out of love. It was more so Julia supporting Mark's walking. "Are you okay?"

"Yeah, yeah, I just need to lay down for a bit," he reassured me.

"Okay well, I'm going to talk to Ms. Delgado and then I'm going to drop off Victoria and Angela. I should be home in an hour or so."

"Sounds good. Drive safe," said Mark.

"I will."

While approaching Ms. Delgado, I gathered together what words to say. As soon as I was a few steps away, an incredibly loud screeching, followed by the sound of a car engine, came roaring down the block toward us. A blue Jeep braked roughly in the front of the courtroom. Without parking, or even closing the door behind him, Angela's dad jumped out of the car and stomped his way towards us, fists clenched and fire in his eyes. "What the hell are you doing here?!" His words traveled past us all and landed right on his daughter. "I...I just wanted to see."

Looking at her, we all witnessed a side of Angela Wilson no one knew existed. One whose hands were shaking and who mumbled over her words. One who couldn't find the confidence, which she normally carried around all day and night. One who had lost her Jimmy. Passersby, both random and from the trial, stopped and became engrossed into the conflict between the two. Nearing her he walked up the steps, reached out, and snatched her wrist. As he began to drag her off, she escaped his grasp quickly and shouted "NO!" now attracting more attention from inside the building.

Letting go of Victoria, I opened my mouth to say something. That was before a sound was emitted from behind me. It resembled the noise of a large sack being dropped against the ground.

"MARK!" Julia's voice screeched through the area. It was as if turning around and noticing Mark slumped over on the ground slowed everything down, except my heartbeat. It raced around the same speed as my steps as I shot over and dropped to the ground. Flipping his body over gently, I twisted my head behind me as far as my neck would let me. "CALL AN AMBULANCE!!" I hollered. I shook his body, looking for some type of response. There was nothing.

***

The stunning light in front of me made my eyes wince. I had no idea what was going on. With the little strength I had I was able to roll my head over to the left of me. It was Jaxson. He was driving, both hands on the steering wheel, and frantically looking back and forth between me and the road. He was talking to me, and by his body language I could tell it was loud. However, I couldn't hear any of it clearly; it was as if my ears were clogged. I slowly returned my head to its position. My head felt like someone was beating upon it with drumsticks. A little bit of rest was all I needed. Closing my eyes, I let my mind drift away.

"*Do you think one day we'll get out of here?*" Julia sat across from me wearing her favorite brown leather coat with a fur hood. Biting her lips, she was eager for my response.

"*I mean, if you wanted to eat somewhere else all you had to do was ask,*" I bantered, as if I didn't know what she really meant. "You know what I mean," she rolled her eyes. "We always talk about it. You even said traveling the world is the first thing you wanted to do after graduation. Well, that was two years ago." She was right after all. It was all I thought about day and night. In my mind I just always thought I would be alone, throughout it all. Julia has always been there, and one thing I loved about her is that she wanted to see the world just as much as I did. Sitting up I picked up one singular French fry and held it up. "One year," I said. "We'll work for one more year and save up as much as we can and then we'll leave. Just me, you, and the road."

"Are you serious?" Her face instantly brightened up, triggering her gorgeous dimples to expose themselves.

"I promise."

***

"I'm truly sorry for you both, but there's nothing more that can be done." The words cut like a dagger across my body. It was ironic how I knew this would come, and even though I thought about it every day, I was still unprepared. I'd tried to ignore this day as much as I'd been trying to ignore the new Mark I'd borne witness to. Not the miserable drunk that tore down everything he could find. The kind, loving one that had always been there, just buried underneath all of the bottles he'd opened. If only we had met earlier.

I could only imagine how many memories we would've made together. Unfortunately it was time for the end of a story, our story. The one that barely began. The man that towered above me in a doctor's gown continued talking and none of it registered in my ears. My mind was two doors down in an all-white room with a man lying on his deathbed. "When can we see him?" Julia spoke up behind us. Her usual pale face was now burning red after hearing the disturbing news.

"Ma'am, I don't-"

"I want to see him!" she shot out, slamming her foot to the ground a bit. A few background conversations that could slightly be heard down the hall stopped. I could feel a couple of glances targeting us. She dug the inside of her fist onto the lower part of her face, which covered her mouth and caught her tears. The doctor glanced down, closed his eyes momentarily, and took a short breath. "Let me consult with the nurses and we'll see what we can do." After he walked away, Julia began to pace back and forward along the width of the hall. After planting my forearm against the hospital wall I dug my head into it.

This was happening
This was happening
This was happening

No matter how many times I replayed it in my head I didn't find the words valid.

Why did he have to start being good? Why did he change if this was going to happen? Surely if I still hated him, this process would've been much easier. Closing my eyes, I focused on my memories. Bringing back any day, event, or moment that was ruined at the hands of Mark. And although a plentiful amount resurfaced, none compared to the times he'd sat across from me and made cheesy jokes. I'd learned more about him in the past five months than I had in my years of living with him. And just when things were falling into place this had to happen? It was as if I lost every parent figure I had in the years I needed them the most.

After roughly thirty or so minutes of sitting in impatience, a buzzing sound came from my pocket. The caller ID read "Victoria" and I instantly remembered how I'd promised her and Angela a ride home. After answering I instantly put the phone to my ear. "Hey, I'm so sorry I forgot about the ride I promised. I just got caught up with the ambulance. Did you two get home safe?" I rushed the apology out of my mouth first, out of guilt for leaving her at the scene. "No, don't even worry about it, you're fine. Jimmy's mom offered to drop me off and Angela's dad took her home. So… how is he doing?" There was no easy way to say this. "He doesn't have much time left." She became silent, which was understandable considering the load I'd just dropped on her.

"Jaxson…I'm sorry I-" My attention shifted from her to the nurse, who was now walking up to Julia and I with a clipboard in hand and a stethoscope around her neck. "Hey, I'm going to have to call you back. Is that okay?"

"Yes, definitely."

"Okay, just let me know when you're home."

After hanging up I stood in anticipation for the news.

***

"Thanks Ms. Delgado, You're a life-saver." I'm pretty sure she took those words with a grain of salt before she told me it was fine and pulled off. Little did she know how true it was. Knowing what Jaxson was going through, Angela's dad taking her and leaving so soon, and the fact that my own father probably wouldn't have even answered the call left me with basically no options. I couldn't blame Jaxson or Angela; it wasn't their faults, and everything did happen so fast after all. Jimmy's mother, like him, was incredibly humble. She was kind and treated the trailer park I lived in as if it were any suburban house, something that's uncommon nowadays.

I watched as her early 2000s Toyota Camry slowly made its way through the dirt tracks. The sounds of her tires collided against the bumpy terrain and startled some of the dogs who were either sleeping or just laying around. In return a chain effect of different dogs, all shapes and sizes, began to bark loudly. This was one of the many reasons I hated staying here. Turning around I made it to the trailer's entrance and unlocked the door. The insides seemed a bit gloomier today. One of the light bulbs had gone out, and I made a mental note to replace it tomorrow. To satisfy the growling in my stomach I opened up our last, packaged, loaf of bread and opened up the refrigerator to clarify whether I would be making a turkey sandwich or a PB&J. Stunned by what I found, I released my grasp of the door and let it fly open.

The refrigerator's interior, which used to at least hold a small amount of food, was completely empty. This had never happened before. I wanted to ask my father about it, but it was peaceful around here for once and I wanted to keep it that way for at least a little while longer. I guessed ravioli would have to do. Opening up the cabinet I was shocked to find out that there was none left. Actually, there was nothing inside. Now worried, I opened the next one and the one after that and the one after that. All of them came up the same - empty. As much as I didn't want to, my last resort was to knock on his door. Hesitant to do so, however, I left my fist hanging inches apart from the dirty white door. Mustering some courage I cocked back slightly and delicately knocked upon the door three consecutive times.

Moments passed and nothing happened; I didn't even hear him shuffle around a bit. I repeated the process two more times, taking a minute's pause in between. Even though I knew for a fact it was most likely locked, I still placed one hand on the knob and slowly twisted it to the right. Peeking through, all I could see was an empty mattress. Swinging the door open, I surveyed the room. Each of his dresser drawers was open and empty, all of his shoes had disappeared from their usual spots, and the TV had vanished, leaving only its dusty outline on the table. We had been robbed. In a fraction of a section I whipped around and burst open my room door. What? This made no sense. On one hand I was happy my room was left untouched, on the other this made no sense. Why would they only take his stuff? Unless...No...he wouldn't.

Would he? Turning around I speed-walked out of my room, down our short hallways leading to our kitchen/living room, and out the front door. His car, which had always been home around this time for the past seven years, was gone. Flipping out my phone I scrolled down to my dad's number and called him. It immediately went to voicemail. I tried again. Nothing. I began to call him frantically over and over. Each time went straight to voicemail. He was gone. No note or anything explaining why. How could he do this? Grabbing handfuls of hair in my hand I began to panic, not only because he'd disappeared, but because I had nowhere else to go. The only hope I had was my mother, who I hadn't called or texted in about a year or so. I clicked on her name, put the phone to my ear, and waited for her to pick up.

***

"Wait, slow down. Where are you now?" Jaxson jumped out of his seat with a look of concern. I had no idea who it was or what was going on. His demeanor screamed that something was wrong. "Are you serious?!" He held his phone to his shoulder and looked at me. "I'm sorry, it's Victoria. I wish I could stay but she really needs my help. Do you think you'll be fine?"

"Yes, yes go. I'll be fine."

He started jogging his way down the white hallway.

"Drive safe!" I shouted, hoping the words traveled down the hallway enough for him to hear them. Even though he cut a corner and I could no longer see him, the scene of him running down the hall stayed in my mind. I still remembered the day he'd first arrived. He was no taller than five feet, soft curly hair, and was so nervous up he barely was able to get a sentence out. It was no secret that the bad times heavily outweighed the good ones, and that stayed on my mind all day every day. Nonetheless, it was truly a privilege to watch him grow into the man he was today.

"Mrs. Palmer, he's awake if you want to see him." Too busy thinking of Jaxson, I hadn't noticed the nurse who snuck up behind me. "Yes," I said, grazing my hands against my jeans and back to my waist before standing up. She led me towards his room and held the door open for me to enter. The first thing I noticed was a huge window on the opposite side of the room, with its own little sitting area underneath it. The walls were grey and so was the hospital bed. The same bed which comforted Mark. Seeing him like this was heartbreaking, to say the least. It was still unbelievable that this was real. His once brawny chest was now shriveled and frail. Different types of tubes ran down his feeble arms. Was this our ending? He repositioned his head slightly to see me.

His dry lips cracked open as he fixed his mouth to say his first words. His hands separated from the bed and reached out for me.

"I'm sorry baby. I'm so sorry-" as he continued to apologize, I rushed over and calmed his hand with mine. "Shhhhhhhhh, it's okay, it's okay."

"No," his lips quivered, "it's too late now."

"Too late for what?" I leaned in closer to him. He gathered just enough strength to caress my cheek with his hand. "The promise I made to you all those years ago; we were supposed to travel the world together. And our baby. What happened...it was all my fault." I slightly tightened my grip on his hands. "Mark- that was a long time ago….." I struggled to put together the words to make him feel better. What was going to happen to him was inevitable; the last thing I wanted was for this to be on his mind when he goes. His voice was weak, and his breathing was low, "We were young, but those dreams were real." Through the struggle he was able to let off a smile.

"Where's Jaxson?" I thought about Jaxson and the truth we owed him. "He had some type of emergency, he left about 5 minutes ago." Mark opened his mouth, "Promise me you'll have him here tomorrow. I have to be the one to tell him."

"I promise."

Chapter 25

My headlights guided us through the ill-light roads. She sat in the front passenger seat and had her head on the glass. She still had on the same yellow dress shirt and dark blue jeans from earlier. Her eyes never left her feet, even as a small teardrop escaped and dropped from her chin. My plan was to take her to my house and then ask her what happened when we got there. As much as I tried to stick to it, I couldn't bear seeing her the way she was now.

"What happened?"

I took a glance over at her before quickly returning my eyes back to the road ahead of us.

"He's gone."

What did that mean?

"Is he hurt? Or like in trouble?"

"No..." I'd never heard her voice this low before. "He left. No note or anything explaining why."

It took a moment for me to process those words correctly. He just left? How could anyone do that to their kid?

"Did you try and contact your mom?"

"I did. Some random man answered the phone. He said it'd been his new number for months now."

During our moment of silence I struggled not only to find the words to say, but also to believe that something as horrible as this could happen to someone like her.

"For a while now I've been trying to figure out why she left. I thought it was something to do with her and not me. Now that he's left, I've realized that it's not them." She faced left towards me, and exposed her streaming face. "It's me; something's wrong with me." After hearing this I immediately pulled over on the nearest sidewalk I could find. I unbuckled my seatbelt and reached over to her side. Placing my hand on both sides of her she got louder, screaming, "It's my fault! It's my fault!" with a cracking voice and waving her hands around, hitting the seat behind her. "No, no, no. Listen to me!" I shouted, hoping it would get her to stop.

"Nothing's wrong with you, they left you because they're screwed up. Not you." I brought my thumb up and wiped away a tear that was beginning to form. "You're perfect. I've known it since the moment we first met, and I know it now." I put her head on my chest and brushed her hair behind her head as she let it all out. We stayed there for a little while longer before I finished taking her to my place. When exiting, I made sure not to wake her up by closing the door as silently as I could. I walked up the stairs and unlocked the front door, before going back and waking her up and letting her know we were there.

Well, that was until I saw how peaceful she looked when she slept. Deciding that her sleep was a temporary relief to her problems, I didn't want to wake her. Placing my forearms behind her back and under her legs I slowly carried her to the house, using the heel of my shoe to close both my car door and the front door. I winced when accidentally hitting a creak on my way up the stairs; luckily, she was still sound asleep. Arriving at my room, I walked inside and gently laid her down in my bed. I guessed I would sleep on the couch - I needed some time to reflect on today anyway. Moving my hands to the end of the bed, I pulled up my covers and slowly wrapped them over her, stopping at the top of her shoulder. The open curtains allowed moonlight to pass through and land on her. Bending over, I planted a kiss on her forehead. I was just about to turn around and head downstairs when I felt her hand stop me.

"Stay. Please stay." Hearing this I didn't think twice before crawling into bed behind her and putting the cover over us both. We lay on our sides and I felt pretty awkward while doing this. Even with the rough night we'd had, I wouldn't trade where I was for the world. The smell of, what I assumed to be, her coconut shampoo made me take in deep breaths, savoring all of it. I wanted nothing more than to make her feel better; if only I knew what words to say. That was when three of the purest, most truthful ones I could think of came to mind. Whether this was the right time or not, it didn't change the fact that I meant them with everything inside of me. I reached one of my hands across her body and cuddled up next to her.

Lifting my head up from the pillow I leaned in a bit next to her ear. "I love you, Victoria." I whispered the words with no idea if she'd heard them or not, nor did it matter. I returned my head to its position. Shortly after she turned around and faced me, eyes open. "Did you really mean that?" she asked in a low tone. "Of course." She moved her lips up and kissed me. A magical kiss which I never wanted to end. We separated and she placed her hand on my heart. "I love you too." She curled into my chest and I embraced her while staring up at my room ceiling. If I had a dollar for everything that seemed to be going wrong in our lives, I think I'd never have to work in life. But for some reason, as shitty as everything was going, being with her calmed every troubling thought in my head. We had no idea what our futures held in store for us. As long as we had each other we'd be just fine.

Waking up in the morning with her in my arms was definitely one of the top ten most satisfying moments of my life. It was something I could for sure get used to, and it was past due. When people would say someone their significant other "slept beautifully" I never understood it; that was until I witnessed it firsthand. Her hair, along with half of her body, had overlapped mine in our sleep. I moved my hand toward her face with the motive of waking her. She looked so tranquil I couldn't bring myself to do it, nor did I ever really want to. The only problem with a time like this was that we would have to eventually leave this bed and face the rest of our disastrous lives.

"I can't stay here for much longer." Too distracted in my own thoughts I hadn't even noticed that Victoria had awoken from her sleep. "Where will you go?" I prayed it wouldn't be too far away. "The only place I can. A foster home." Lifting my head and shoulders up I laid my back against my bedpost, staring straight at the closet in front of me. "I have no other relatives. And no money for the rent." Homeless; she was going to be homeless. The most passionate, understanding, and magical person I'd ever met was going to suffer at such a young age, solely from pure unluckiness. "What if you stayed here?" Several moments of stillness brushed through the air. "I couldn't." I curled my fingers underneath her chin, and guided her head up to meet mine.

"You can, you just don't want to."

"I can't."

"Oh come on, would a couple of days really hurt?" I folded my arms and put on the best convincing look I had.

"I'll admit, I wouldn't mind waking up to this…but what would they say?"

Hearing those words instantly reminded me of yesterday's events. My hands rummaged through the sheets rapidly for my phone. "What's going on, is everything okay?"

"Please help me find my phone. I need to call the hospital." After hearing the word hospital she got off of the bed and started checking the floor. "Here!" She held out the device for me to take. "Thank you," I practically snatched it out of her hands and had already started my call for Julia in a matter of seconds. After two short rings she picked up the phone, "Jaxson." The fact that she answered the phone by saying my name in a concerned tone scared me. Now standing up out of my bed, I observed that Victoria was watching me out of my peripheral vision.

"Is he gone?"

"No... he's just... He-" Her voice sounded broken as she struggled to put her words together.

"He's not well," she managed to get out.

"Look Jaxson, I know he hasn't been great to you, and neither have I. This may be too much to ask for, but we need you today. He needs you." I could hear her voice crack. She sounded desperate, yet truthful. "The doctors say he-- he doesn't have much t-time left. And honestly," I heard a huge sniff come through the phone followed by a gut-wrenching sob, "I feel like he's- holding o-on to talk to you again. Please, please, please, give him a chance. He...he just wants you to understand before it's too late."

"Understand what? You're not making any sense."

"Jaxson!" The phone went silent. A few muffled weeps could be heard. "I need you to be here."

If only I still resented him. If only I was still disgusted with his face this would all be easier. Part of me just wanted to go. Losing him was something I didn't want to remember. Then part of me remembered the words he'd told me in the diner. His words when he gave me the key.

"I've done a lot of things wrong. But if I'm going to die, I at least want to do that right."

I still remembered the look in his eyes when he'd said those words. They weren't the eyes of the man who kicked me out of the house or tore up every single drawing I'd ever made. They were looking for redemption; nothing more, nothing less. And the key. He still hadn't told me what it was for.

"What time are visiting hours?"

"The nurses said around two."

"Okay. I'll be there when I can."

Clicking off the phone, I realized that the pain of loss would soon knock on my door. And living in this house wouldn't make any of it easier. "Is everything okay?" Victoria questioned. "We need to go to the hospital… he's not well."

Chapter 26

"Where is she?"
"Sir, calm down-"
"I need to see her!"

A nurse appeared from the door and stood by its entrance. It felt like she was doing everything in her power to avoid making eye contact. I didn't break my gaze with her, as she didn't break hers from the ground.

"You!" I motioned my head towards her. "Please tell me what's going on." Someone telling me that she and the baby were fine was all I needed. The head injury I'd suffered meant nothing to me at this moment. Only those two. I couldn't lose them how I lost my mother. The fate of my future was sitting behind my door and I had no idea how it looked. The man turned around and stopped at the nurse's feet. She pulled down her surgical mask and leaned forward to whisper in his ear. After a head nod they parted ways. She stepped back into her room and he turned around and approached me. "Sir, she's going to be fine." Relief engulfed my body. My hands dropped to my knees. My breathing slowed down, turning into laughter of joy. One question still hadn't been answered.

My head turned up into the doctor's eyes.
"What about the baby?"
No words left his mouth.
"The baby's fine, right?"
"Sir, I'm sorry. We lost the baby."
"No you didn't."
"Sir-"

"No! You didn't."

It was me. I took the baby from both of us.

"Mark!" *Julia's voice surrounded me. I didn't know what direction it was coming from.* "Wake up!"

The words repeated themselves.

Wake up
Wake up
Wake up
Wake up

The hospital light directly above me blinded my eyes. I tried to move my hands and block the light out, but I wasn't able to do so. Lifting my head up weakly I managed to readjust my head in the pillow. Julia's face was the first thing I could make out in the room. Julia placing her hand on my arm stopped it instantly. "Is he here?" Footsteps from the back corner of the room announced Jaxson's presence. "I'm right here." With everything that had been going on I hadn't acknowledged that he was basically a man now. His lean muscle was vastly different than the scrawny boy we'd adopted. "Give us some alone time." She stood up and exited the room, turning back to look at me one more time.

The truth sets people free. That was all that mattered. "I spent all those years hating you, because I hated myself. I spent weeks finding you through any article or website I could to adopt you. I just wanted to right my wrongs." His eyes squinted a bit, indicating that he was puzzled.

"What are you talking about?" he asked quizzically.

"Julia and I were in the other car that night. I took my eyes off the road for one second and the next thing I knew I woke up in the ambulance." He took a step back. His mouth dropped and his eyes were stuck wide-open. "I wanted to make everything right. But, when I saw your face...I couldn't-"

I felt it. It was like a staleness. It started at my feet, and it was traveling up my spine. Was this what it felt like? No. I still had something to do. "I couldn't handle the guilt. And I tried to lose the feeling by drinking." The fact that this was where I was in life was hard to digest. However, this was my price to pay.

"I carried the pain of it all on me every day. Ruining the lives of the people around me over and over. That's why I refused to fight this when I found out. I thought the world would be better off if I left. And I still think that." He still hadn't said a word. I don't blame him either. The fact that he hadn't walked out or unhooked my breathing machines astonished me. "That key-" My words were interrupted by mucus that rattled up my throat. An extremely dry cough jumped out of my mouth followed by a few more, only getting louder. "There's a -" Breathing was becoming more and more of a struggle the more I talked. I gasped for air. It was like all the oxygen in the room had depleted.

The same flatline noise that screeched through the air the day my mother died had found its way back into my ears. I couldn't move anything in my body. Through my peripheral vision, I could barely make out people storming in the room. One more time. If this was the end, I would like to see her angelic face one more time. My body became completely stale. No matter how many times they talked or touched me, I felt and heard nothing.

My life flashed before my eyes, starting with my earliest memory of my mom giving me a bath. I remembered she would wrestle me because I refused to take my socks off. For some reason I believed that this would protect me from the monster hiding underneath my bed. When she found out about this, she stayed with me every night until I wasn't afraid anymore. Then, I was eighteen again. It was the night of senior prom. She looked beautiful in her turquoise dress as we danced to Elvis Presley's *Can't Help Falling in Love*. It was a moment I'd never forget. After that came the first day I met Jaxson. He wore a yellow shirt and carried a paintbrush with him wherever he went. I took him to the beach the next day. Frightened of the water, he wouldn't go near it unless I held his hand. And finally, it was the moment we were able to get his car up and running. It all allowed me one last smile before the last strand of life left my body.

Chapter 27

He wasn't who I thought he was. For years I thought he was rotten to the core. Now, I knew the truth of Mark. He was funny, wise, and scarred. Unfortunately, like many others, he failed at learning how to accept and move on. That was his downfall. I grasped the urn one more time in my hands before placing it on the counter one last time. It was the most any of us had left of him. I carefully placed it back on the countertop. Saying goodbye is a significant moment that everyone will have to experience at some point. Whether it's to a new-found friend on your first day of kindergarten, or the love of your life. Today was my turn. And although it had been long awaited, I still feel like there's a piece of me that won't be joining Victoria and I on the road today.

"Will you be okay?"

Julia grazed the side of my face. Her vermillion cheeks and black eyes were filled with worry. I'd given my goodbyes to everyone I needed to in Sycamore. From visiting Jimmy to enjoying one last meal at Joe's to finally setting up an appointment with Mrs. Ryan. All I had to do was repeat them one last time to Julia. The uncomplicated task seemed so easy on paper. On the other hand, accomplishing it was a different story. "It's you that I'm worried about." Once I left, Julia would be alone in this house. "No, no, don't worry about me. You've been here long enough, you deserve this." I could hear the trunk slamming behind me. Victoria must've finally been able to fit her wardrobe inside the car, which probably mainly consisted of sweaters.

"I have one more thing to give you before you go. I would've given it to you earlier. The jewelry store had a hard time repairing it." She opened up my hands and placed something inside them. One felt like a thin chain while the other item felt like a card. "I know we took everything from you. That's something we can never make up for. This is the best I can do for now." She let go of my hands, letting me know that it was okay to see what was inside. A stainless silver necklace sat in my palm next to a blue VISA card.

"Is this-"

"Yes, it's the same one your mother had. We wanted to give it to you when we were ready to tell you… and…I'm so-"

Cutting her off, I embraced her. This action wasn't out of guilt or because I felt I needed to. It was truly because I wanted to. For so long I'd drowned every bit of sympathy and compassion I felt for Julia. Now that I knew the truth, I didn't have to anymore. My grasp on her tightened as my eyes burned. I released her from my grip and whipped a forming tear out of my eye socket. "That key he gave you was to a safe full of his life savings. I went ahead and deposited it into a bank account for you…This may be hard to believe, but he loved you." I placed a hand on her shoulder. "I know he did." I never thought I'd say this, but I was going to miss her. Along with Mark and this house. I clenched the necklace in my hand, bringing back so many soothing memories of my mother. "Thank you."

One last nod was all I could offer her before starting up the engine. I always thought that when I left it'd be through my bedroom window and I wouldn't say a word to anyone. Who knew how vastly different it would be? Nonetheless, there was one expectation that was fulfilled. The overwhelming sense of freedom flowing throughout me. And to make things even better, I wasn't alone. Victoria, my shotgun rider, held her hand out the window, letting the wind brush against it. And yet again, she never ceased to amaze me. No matter what the situation was or what was going on, she always looked perfect.

The roads in front of me felt like a void that needed to be filled. Each road held its own adventure; all we had to do was choose one. I hung the phoenix necklace on the car mirror so it would always be in my view. Something was different about this moment. Maybe it was the fact that the artless world around me had color for once, or it was the sun that finally shone down on me through the windshield. One thing I did know was that this was the beginning of a new installment of my life. Looking over at Victoria, I remembered something she'd told me a while ago.

"Hey, don't you have a scrapbook of places you wanted to visit?" Her colored eyes peeked over at me. "Been adding on to it ever since I was twelve," she smiled. "Well, if you ever wanted to pull it out, now's a great time." "Nah," she grinned, and turned her attention back to her window. "We can get to those later."

"And for now?"

She looked over at me. Blessing me with her gorgeous smile and eyes that I wanted to wake up to every morning for the rest of my life.

"Wherever the roads take us."

***

Sold.

I took a nice long stare at the words. Thinking about what they meant. Knowing exactly what would be moving on to someone else. The mournfully quiet two-floor house. I took the last cardboard box and packed it into my trunk. Once inside the driver's seat, I relaxed in the car. Goodbyes are a powerful, yet challenging, thing. To say farewell to the only thing you've known for years. Even if it set you free. I placed the urn containing Mark's remains in the passenger seat, right next to me. I knew it was impractical. I knew he was somewhere far, far away from here. Yet, for some reason, the urn made it feel like he was right here.

Mark wasn't a perfect man. He was more misconceived than anything. Not a lot of people knew that about him. I reached across the seat and brushed my hands down the black and gold capsule. "I'll keep our promise for the both of us," I said before turning the key in the ignition. From there, I let the wheels take us away. I let them take us down California's Pacific Coast Highway and Virginia's Blue Ridge Parkway. I let them take us over the Golden Gate Bridge and off into the sunset. But no matter where they take us, I know I'll never be too far from you. Mark. The love of my life. You will always, and forever, be my husband.

Epilogue

To my Dear Mark,

Goodbyes have always been something I struggled with. And since I won't be around for much longer, I wanted to give you a piece of me that lasts forever. I'd be lying if I told you life's going to be easy. I'd be lying if I told you that being a parent, paying bills, or your father walking out on us wasn't hard. But, I'd also be lying if I told you that having you wasn't the best thing that ever happened to me. Having a kid gave me a chance to be better than I ever was, and I hope that one day you can experience the same.

For 27 years there hasn't been a day where you haven't crossed my mind. There hasn't been a night where I haven't stayed up wondering if you were okay. And there hasn't been a second where I haven't loved you. Since I won't be there, I need you to make a promise. Promise me when you have a kid of your own, you'll never leave their side. Promise you'll teach them everything I taught you. Promise me you'll be there for every event, no matter what the circumstance may be. And promise you'll bless them with unconditional love.

-Love, Mom

Author Notes:

Writing *Wherever The Road Takes Us* was arguably the best thing I've ever done with my life. It's astounding how much you can learn about life just by creating one out of thin air. Even though these characters and stories are fiction, they hold a tangible place in my heart. Spending hours in a dark room going on a journey with these characters has made me a better person. Each of the characters in this book represents a piece of me. Jaxson's the part of me that realized I have an entire life ahead of me, with no idea what it will look like. Jimmy's the embodiment of my fear of letting those around me down. And Victoria is the writer in me that finally set itself free.

www.ingramcontent.com/pod-product-compliance
Lightning Source LLC
LaVergne TN
LVHW091545060526
838200LV00036B/712